·THE· HISTRONAUTS

A ROMAN ADVENTURE

Written by
FRANCES DURKIN

Illustrated by
GRACE COOKE

Designed by
VICKY BARKER

JOLLY FiSH PRESS

Text © Frances Durkin 2017
Illustrations © Grace Cooke 2017

Book design by Vicky Barker
Illustrations by Grace Cooke

First published in the United Kingdom by b small publishing ltd.

Published in the United States by Jolly Fish Press, an imprint of North Star Editions, Inc.

First US Edition
First US Printing, 2019

This is a work of fiction. Names, characters, places, and incidents are either the product of the author's imagination or are used fictitiously, and any resemblance to actual persons living or dead, business establishments, events, or locales is entirely coincidental.

Library of Congress Cataloging-in-Publication Data (pending)
978-1-63163-244-0 (paperback)
978-1-63163-243-3 (hardcover)

Jolly Fish Press
North Star Editions, Inc.
2297 Waters Drive
Mendota Heights, MN 55120
www.jollyfishpress.com

Printed in the United States of America

Contents

Meet
The Histronauts

Luna

Age: Eight years
Likes: History, adventures, animals, problem solving, and storytelling
Dislikes: Getting lost and bad smells
Favorite Color: Blue
Favorite Food: Beans on toast
Favorite Place: Castles

Nani

Age: Seven and a half years
Likes: Science, nature, math, gardening, flowers, and exploring
Dislikes: People who don't recycle
Favorite Color: Green
Favorite Food: Anything green
Favorite Place: Anywhere outside but mostly forests

Newton

Age: Ten years
Likes: Making things, eating, reading, cooking, and playing games
Dislikes: Being hungry and being cold
Favorite Color: Yellow
Favorite Food: Everything!
Favorite Place: Home

Hero

Age: Five years
Likes: Sleeping, being Luna's cat
Dislikes: Getting wet
Favorite Food: Chicken
Favorite Place: Curled up on the sofa

Timeline

753 BC
Romulus builds the city of Rome. It is a kingdom and the leaders are kings.

509 BC
Rome becomes a republic. The leaders are now elected politicians called senators.

45 BC
Julius Caesar takes over Rome from the senators and ends the republic.

27 BC
The Roman Empire is now very large. The new leader is an emperor.

AD 117
The Roman Empire is at its peak.

AD 395
Rome splits into Eastern and Western Empires.

AD 476
The Roman Empire ends.

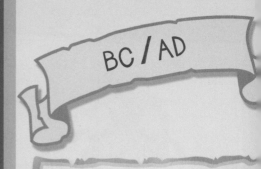

BC / AD

- Planet Earth is over four billion years old.

- Historians divide these years into two time periods, which they call BC or AD.

- The BC dates come first and count down to 1 BC, then the AD dates start and count up from AD 1 to today.

- The current year is an AD year.

- These dates help historians know when things happened.

An ordinary game becomes a great adventure

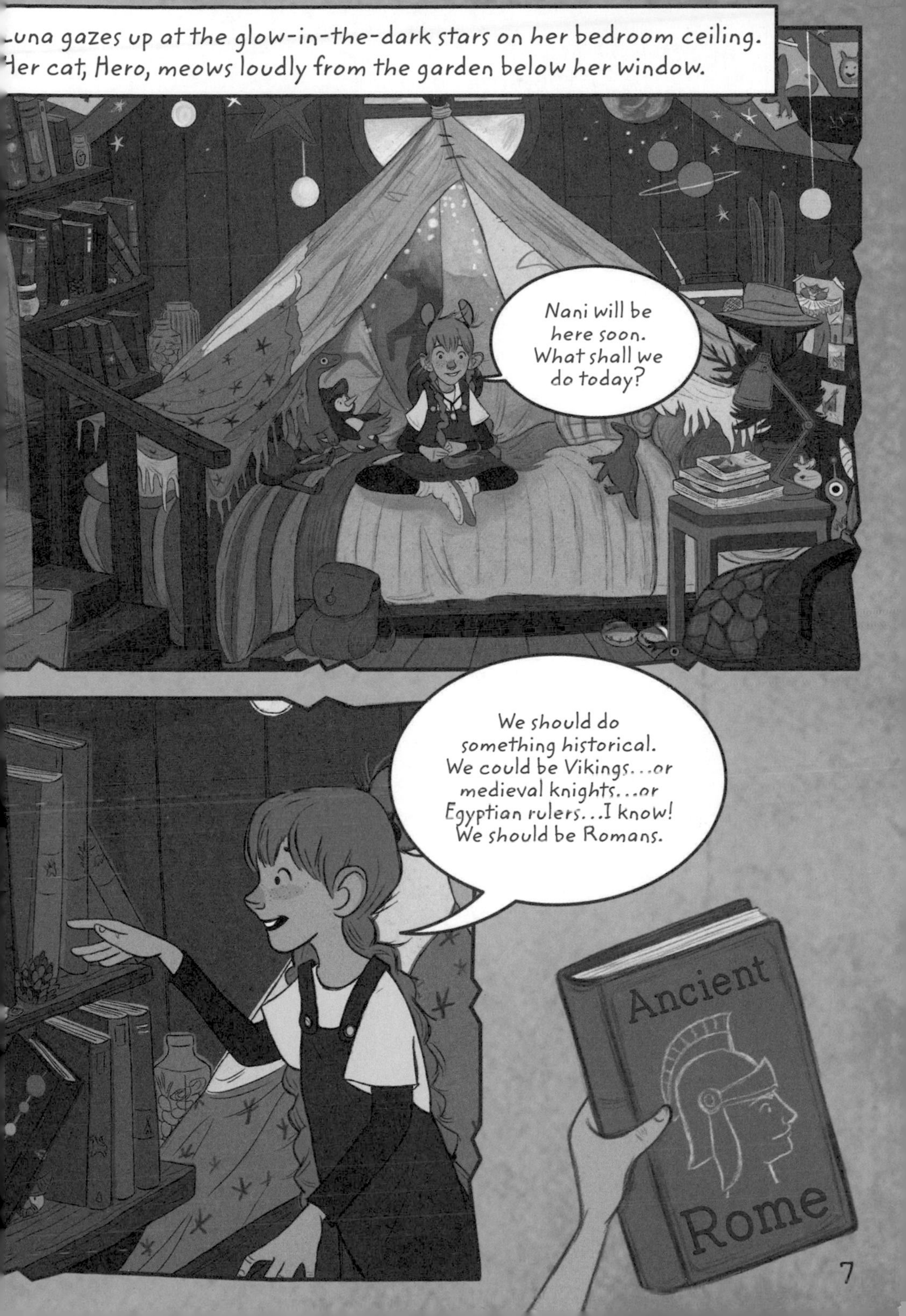

Luna gazes up at the glow-in-the-dark stars on her bedroom ceiling. Her cat, Hero, meows loudly from the garden below her window.
Nani will be here soon. What shall we do today?
We should do something historical. We could be Vikings...or medieval knights...or Egyptian rulers...I know! We should be Romans.
Ancient Rome

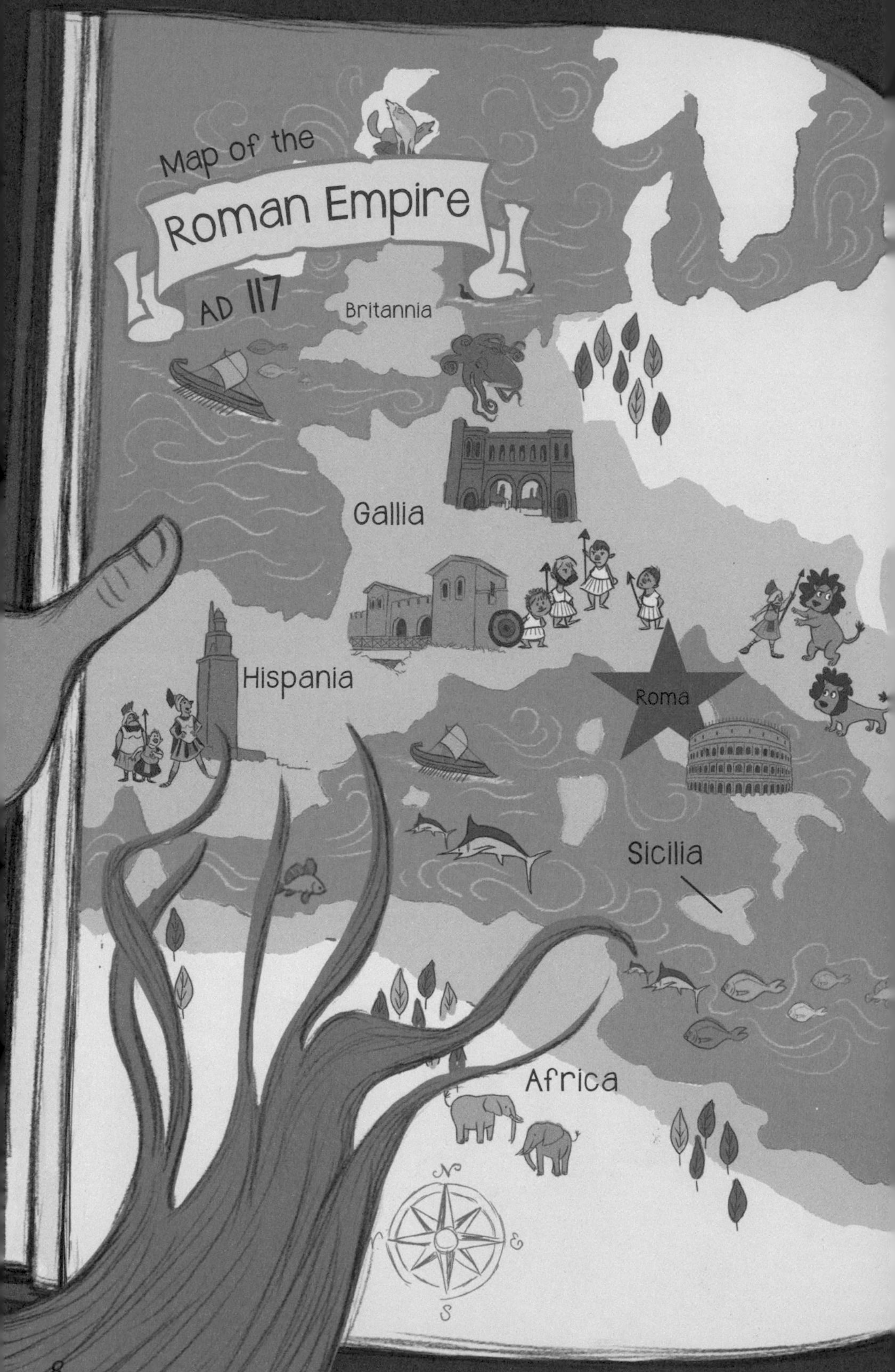
Map of the
Roman Empire
AD 117
Britannia
Gallia
Hispania
Roma
Sicilia
Africa
N
E
S

The Legend of Romulus and Remus

There was a king who had twin nephews named Romulus and Remus. The king was afraid that the boys would turn against him, so he left them beside a river to die. A she-wolf found them and fed them until a shepherd took care of them. When they grew up the twins decided to create a city but argued over where to build it. In their fight, Remus was killed. Romulus built the city on his own and he named it Rome.

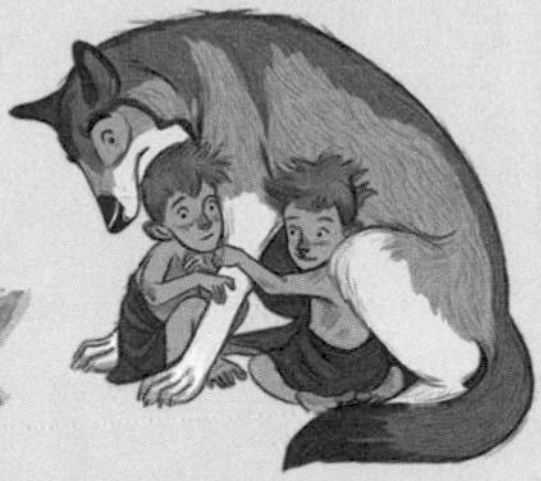

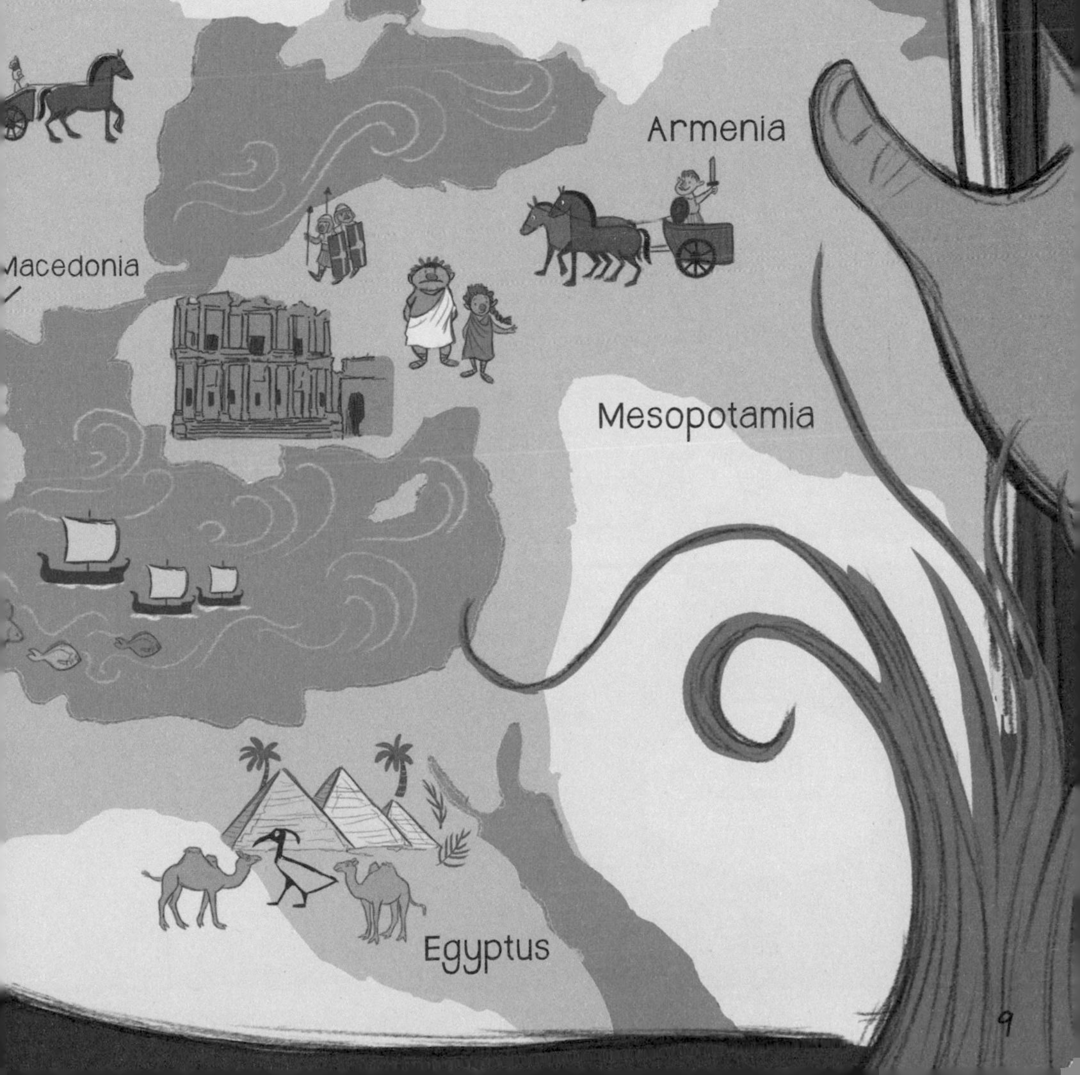
Armenia
Macedonia
Mesopotamia
Egyptus

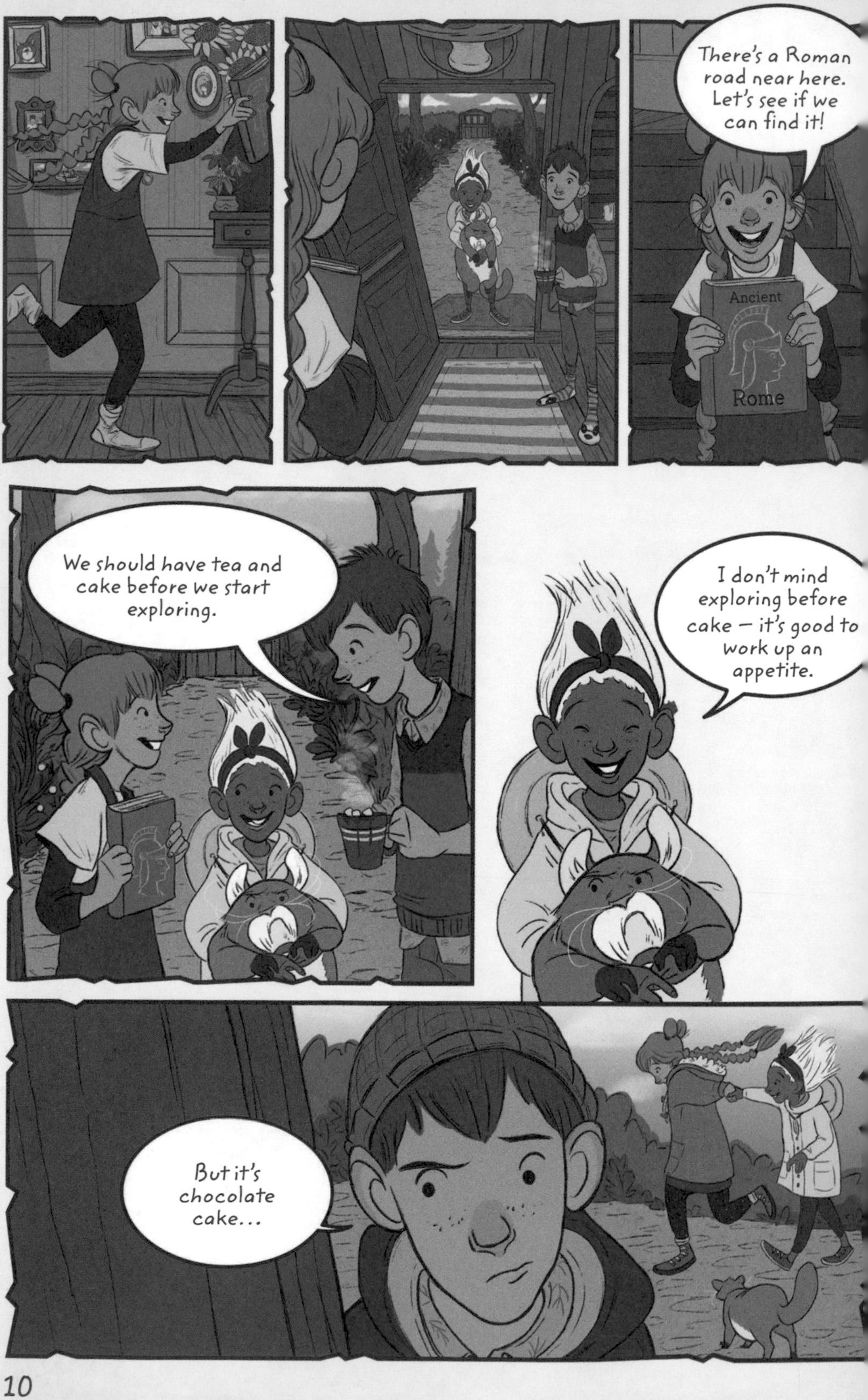
There's a Roman road near here. Let's see if we can find it!
Ancient Rome
We should have tea and cake before we start exploring.
I don't mind exploring before cake – it's good to work up an appetite.
But it's chocolate cake...

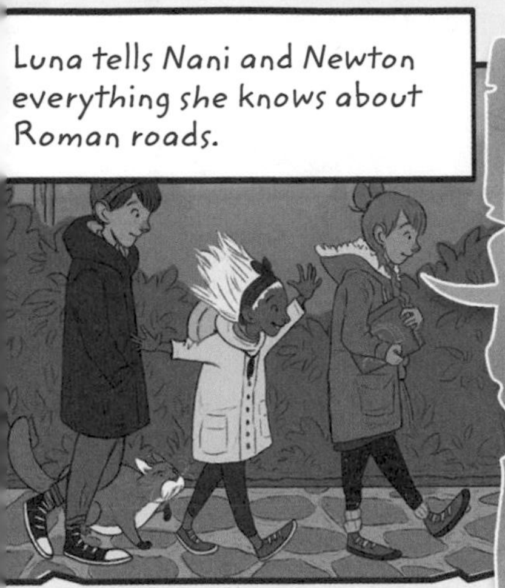
Luna tells Nani and Newton everything she knows about Roman roads.

Did you know?

- The Romans built nearly 53,000 miles (85,300 km) of long, straight roads all over Europe.
- They made the roads from stone. The roads sloped into ditches at either side so that rainwater would drain away.
- Straight roads were faster to move along than bendy ones. Straight roads also made it easier for the huge number of soldiers in the army to march to places.
- People would travel along the roads either by walking, riding in chariots, or in carts pulled by oxen.
- Some of today's roads run in the same places as roads that the Romans built more than 2,000 years ago.

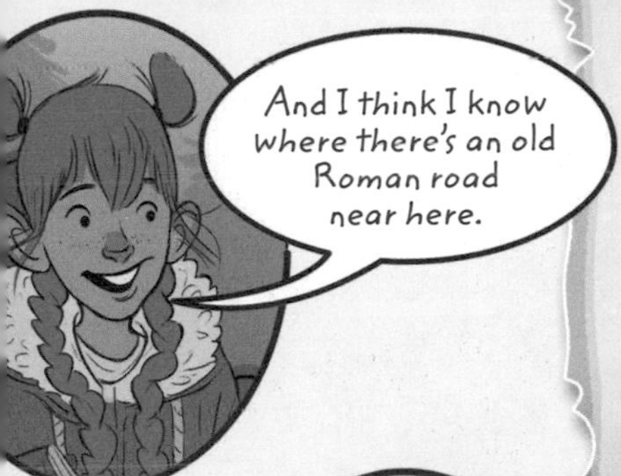
And I think I know where there's an old Roman road near here.

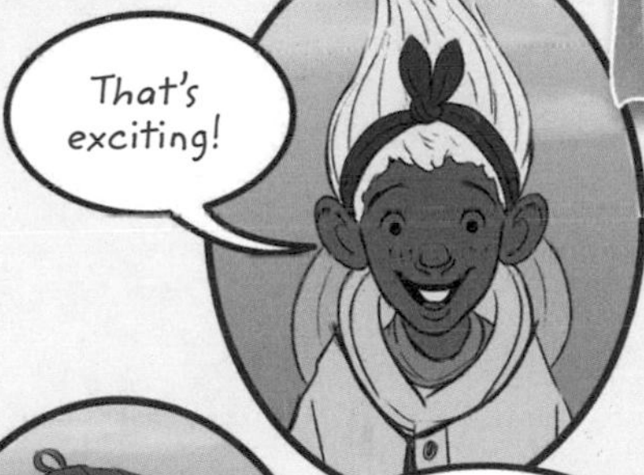
That's exciting!

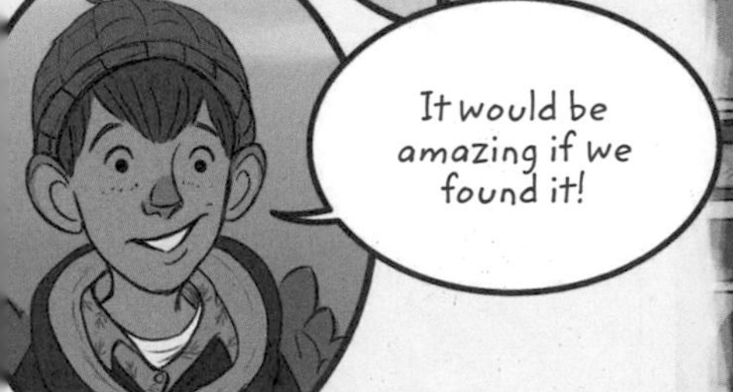
It would be amazing if we found it!

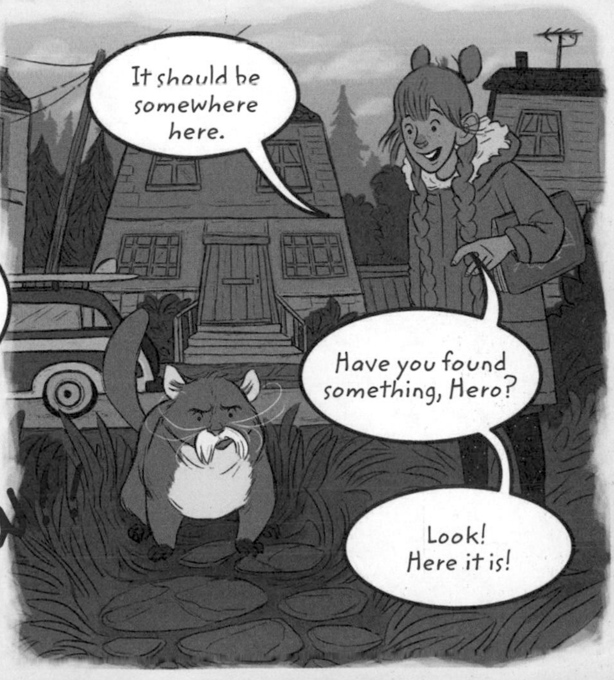
It should be somewhere here.
MEEEOOOOW!
Have you found something, Hero?
Look! Here it is!

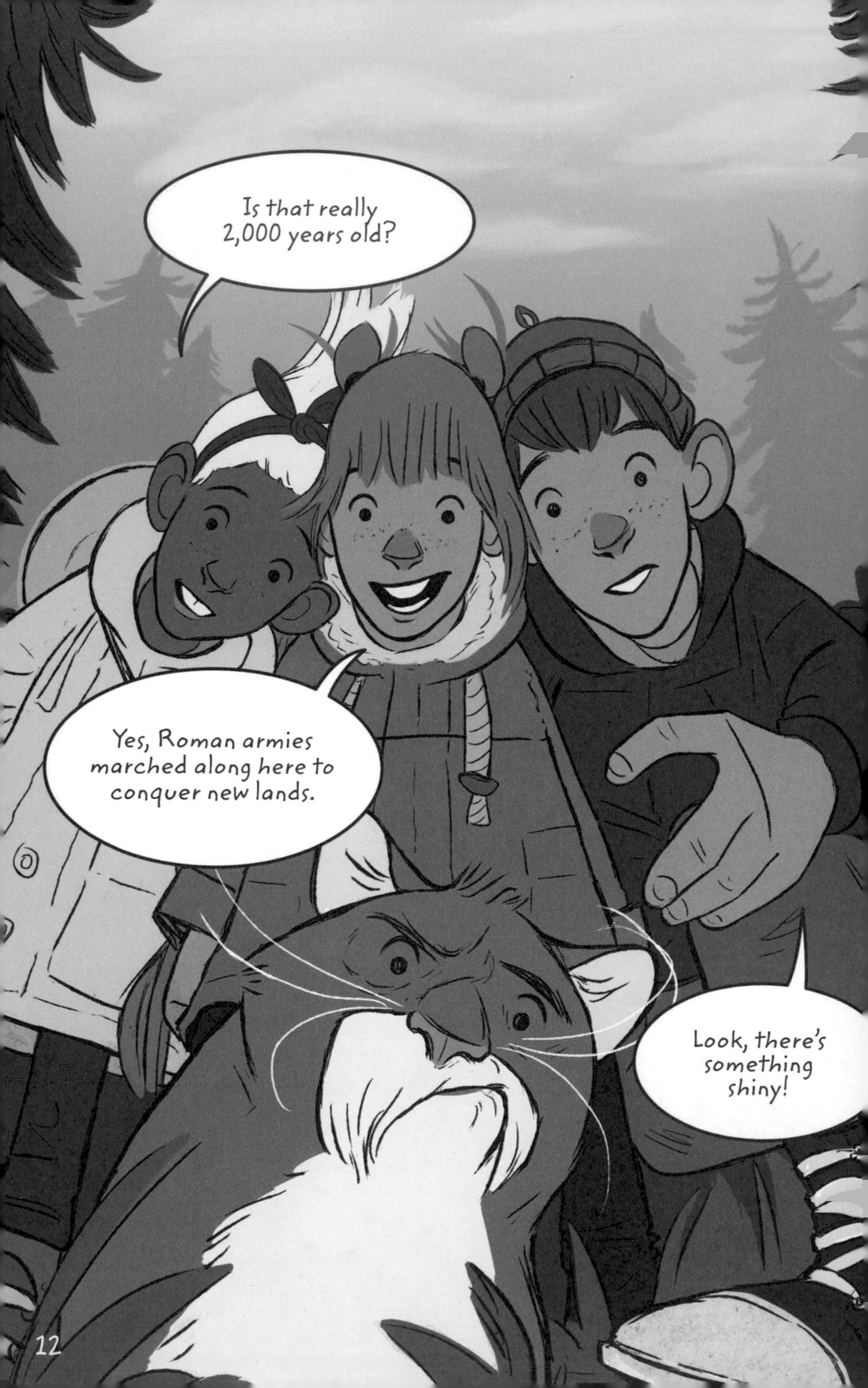
Is that really 2,000 years old?
Yes, Roman armies marched along here to conquer new lands.
Look, there's something shiny!

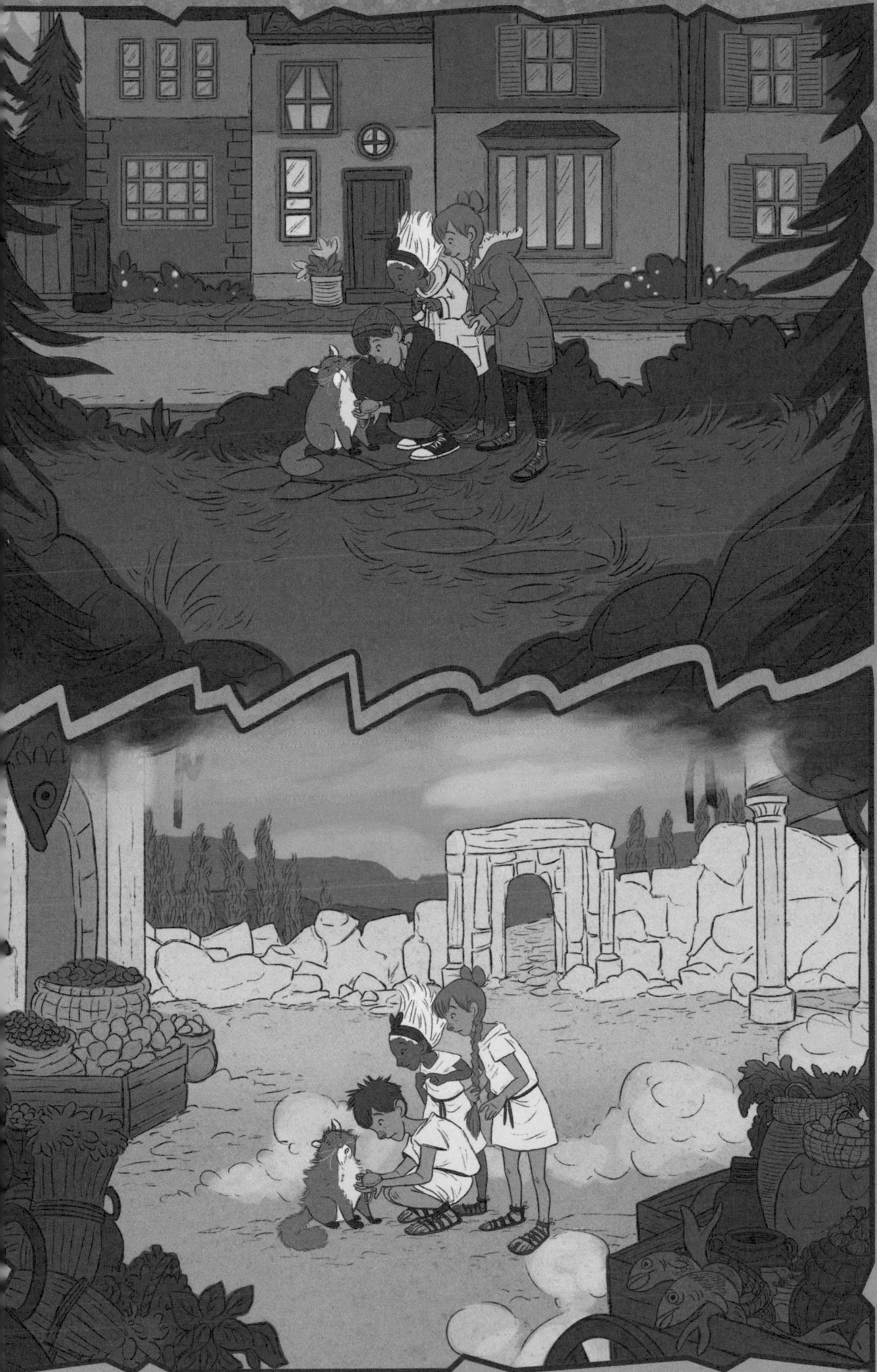

A new friend from a different time

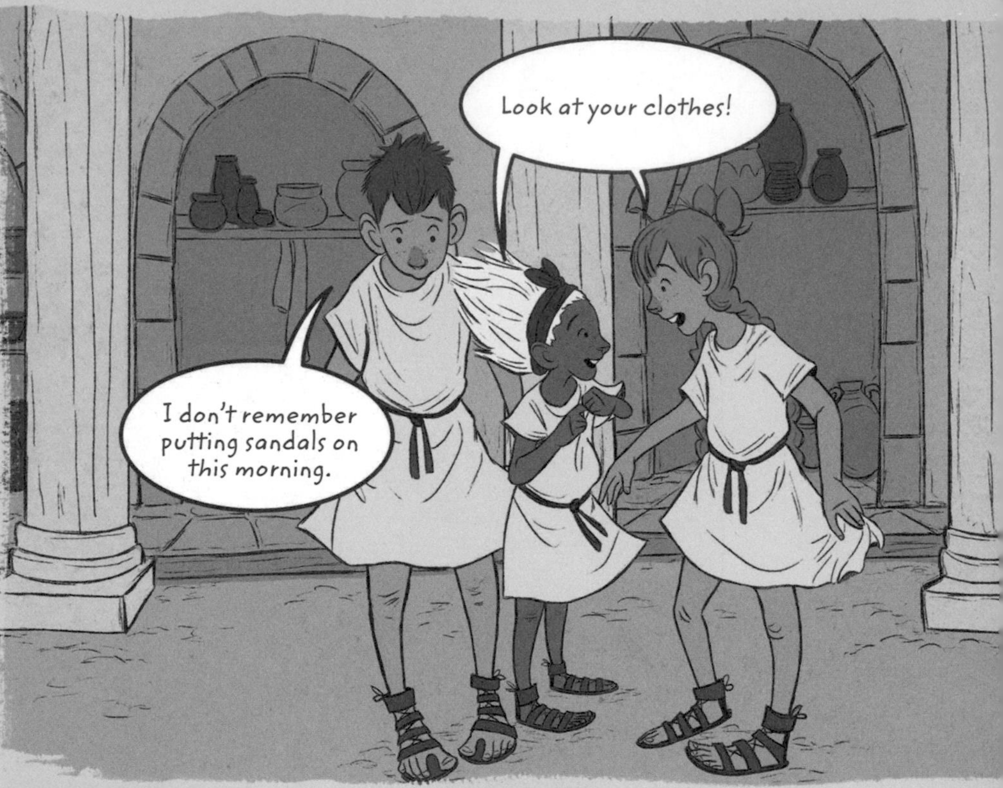
Look at your clothes!
I don't remember putting sandals on this morning.

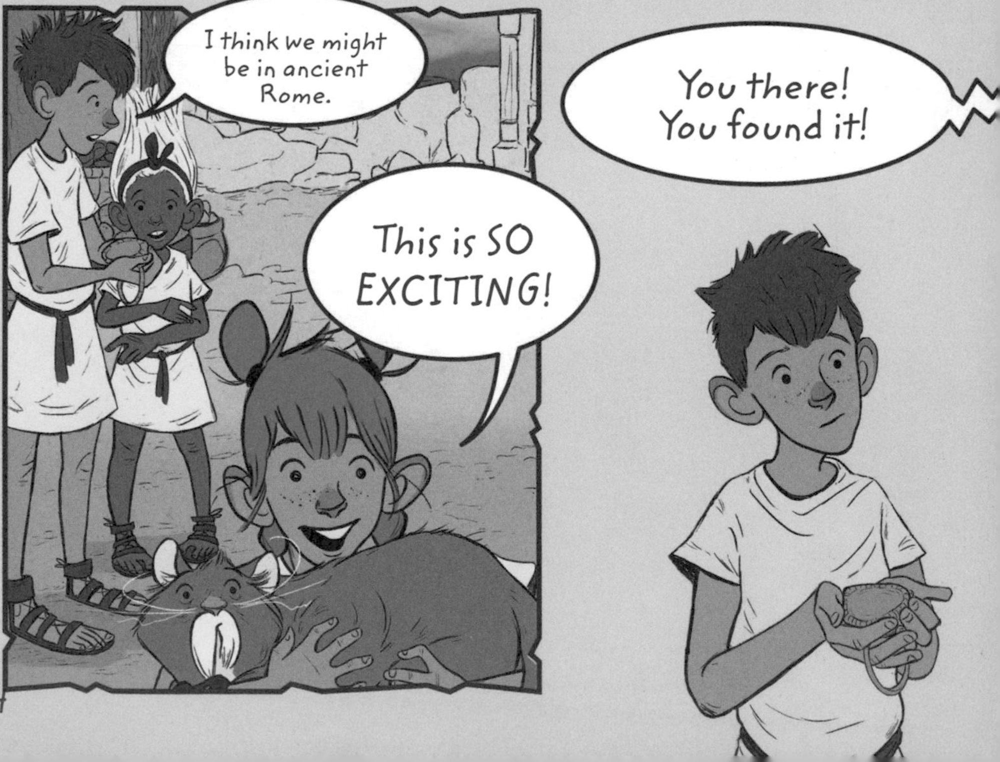
I think we might be in ancient Rome.
This is SO EXCITING!
You there! You found it!

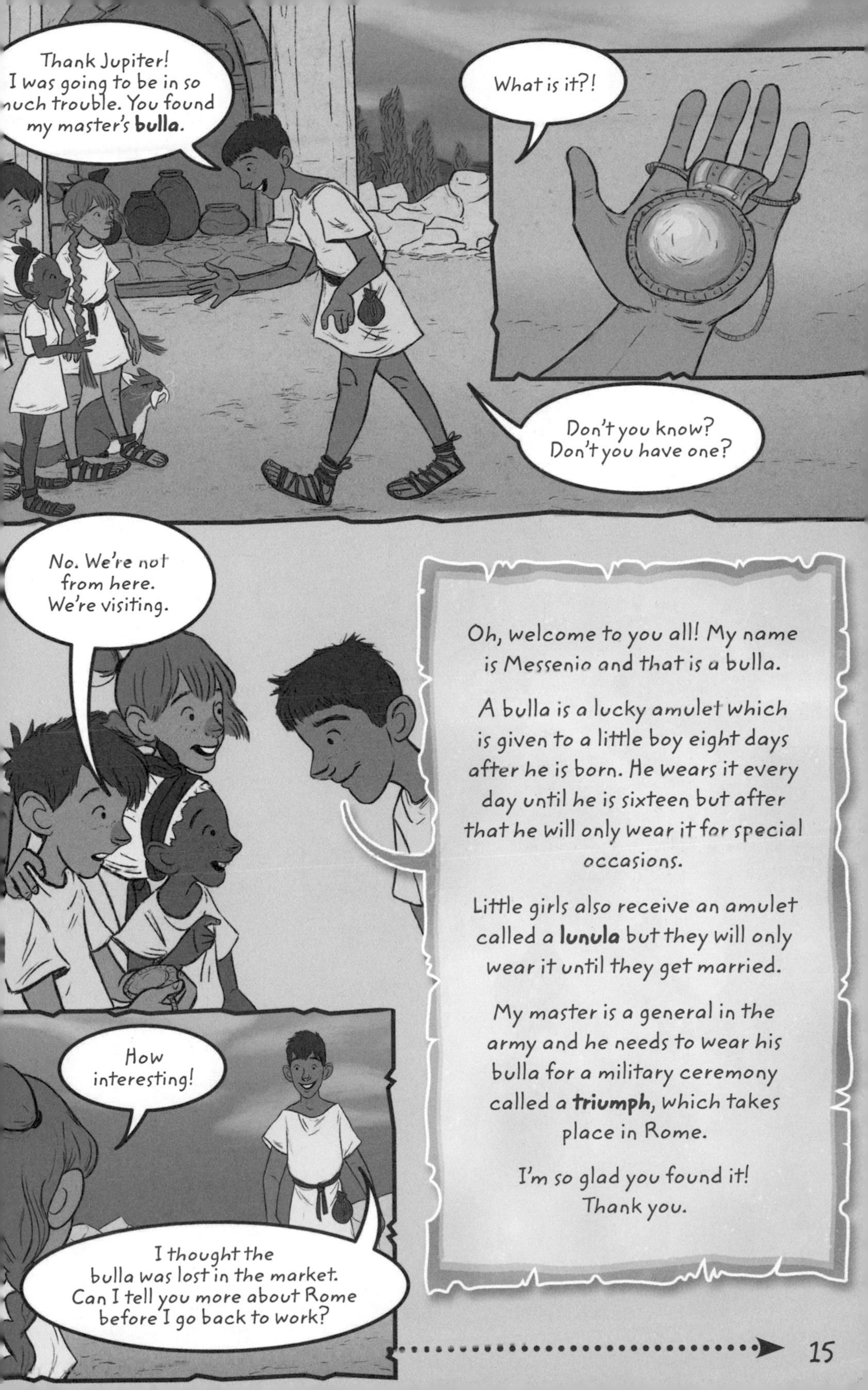

Thank Jupiter! I was going to be in so much trouble. You found my master's **bulla**.
What is it?!
Don't you know? Don't you have one?
No. We're not from here. We're visiting.
Oh, welcome to you all! My name is Messenio and that is a bulla.
A bulla is a lucky amulet which is given to a little boy eight days after he is born. He wears it every day until he is sixteen but after that he will only wear it for special occasions.
Little girls also receive an amulet called a **lunula** but they will only wear it until they get married.
My master is a general in the army and he needs to wear his bulla for a military ceremony called a **triumph**, which takes place in Rome.
I'm so glad you found it! Thank you.
How interesting!
I thought the bulla was lost in the market. Can I tell you more about Rome before I go back to work?

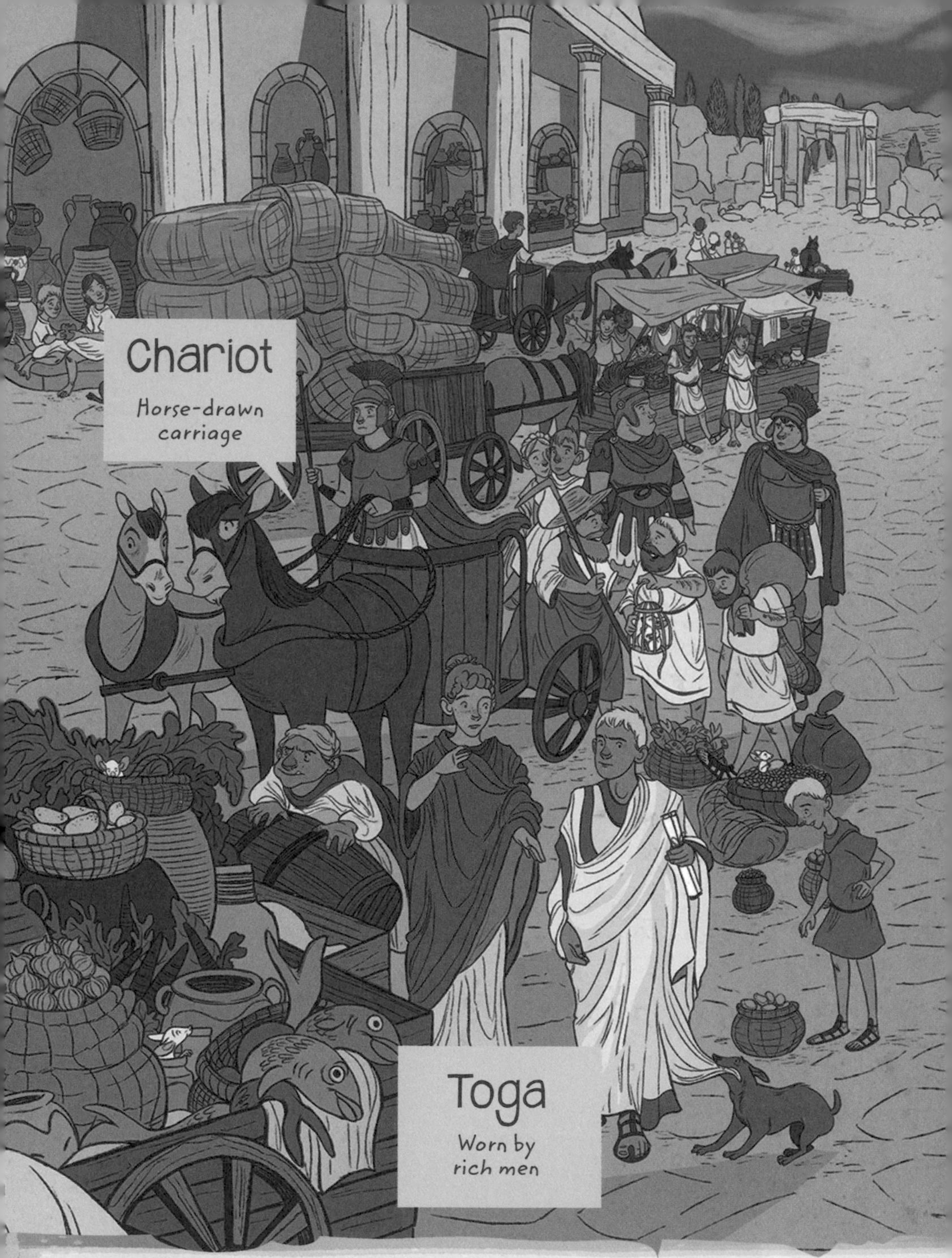
Chariot
Horse-drawn carriage
Toga
Worn by rich men

Can you find these objects in the busy market scene?

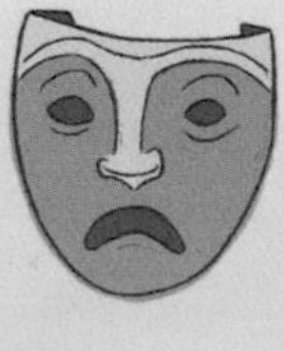

1 theater mask

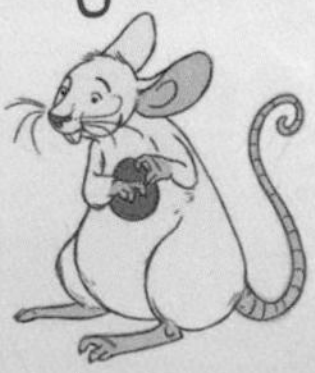

7 mice

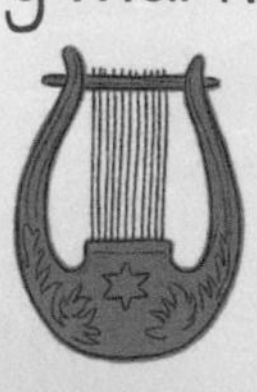

2 lyres

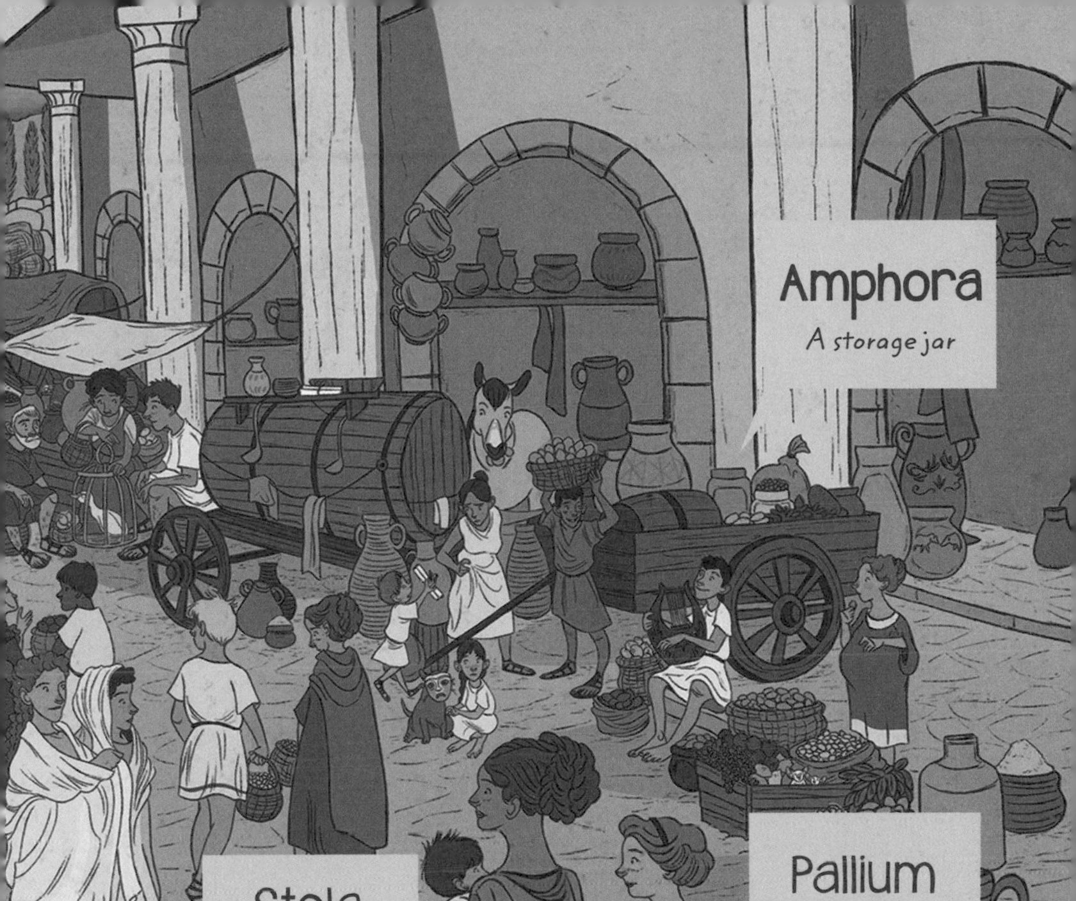
Amphora
A storage jar
Pallium
A woolen cloak
Stola
Dress worn by women
Sandals
Leather shoes worn by men, women, and children

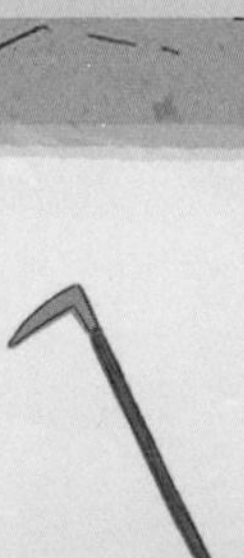

1 farm tool

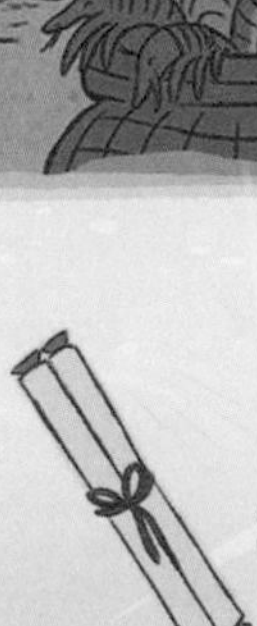

3 scrolls

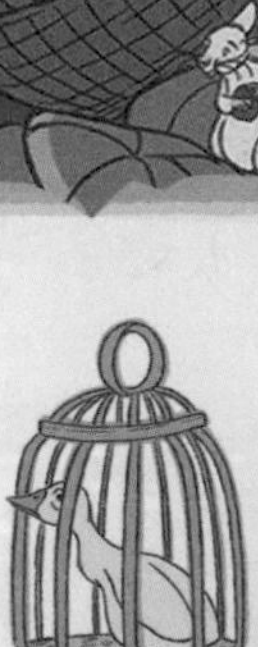

1 bird in a cage

Messenio, please could we come with you to see the city?

I'd love to show you where I live but I am a slave and I have to finish my work for my master.

A slave?!

People buy and sell slaves at markets all over the Roman Empire. Some are born slaves and some slaves are the prisoners who were captured in Roman wars.

A slave is forced to do lots of different types of jobs such as teacher, miner, cook, or even gladiator. They have no choice.

Roman masters own their slaves so they do not pay them for their work, but if a slave works hard for thirty years, or saves up enough money, he or she can ask to be free. A free slave is known as a **libertus** and can become a Roman citizen who is allowed to vote.

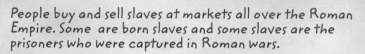

It's illegal to keep people as slaves where we come from. Are we allowed to help you?

I have so much to finish before my master's ceremony. Keep me company as I work.

You can keep the bulla safe. A bulla belongs to a boy so you must look after it, Newton. It's very important.

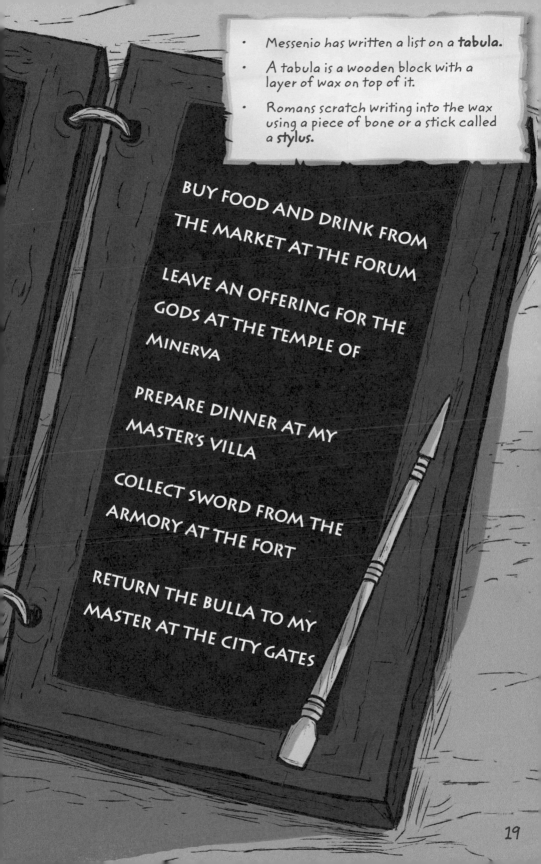

- Messenio has written a list on a **tabula.**
- A tabula is a wooden block with a layer of wax on top of it.
- Romans scratch writing into the wax using a piece of bone or a stick called a **stylus.**

BUY FOOD AND DRINK FROM THE MARKET AT THE FORUM

LEAVE AN OFFERING FOR THE GODS AT THE TEMPLE OF MINERVA

PREPARE DINNER AT MY MASTER'S VILLA

COLLECT SWORD FROM THE ARMORY AT THE FORT

RETURN THE BULLA TO MY MASTER AT THE CITY GATES

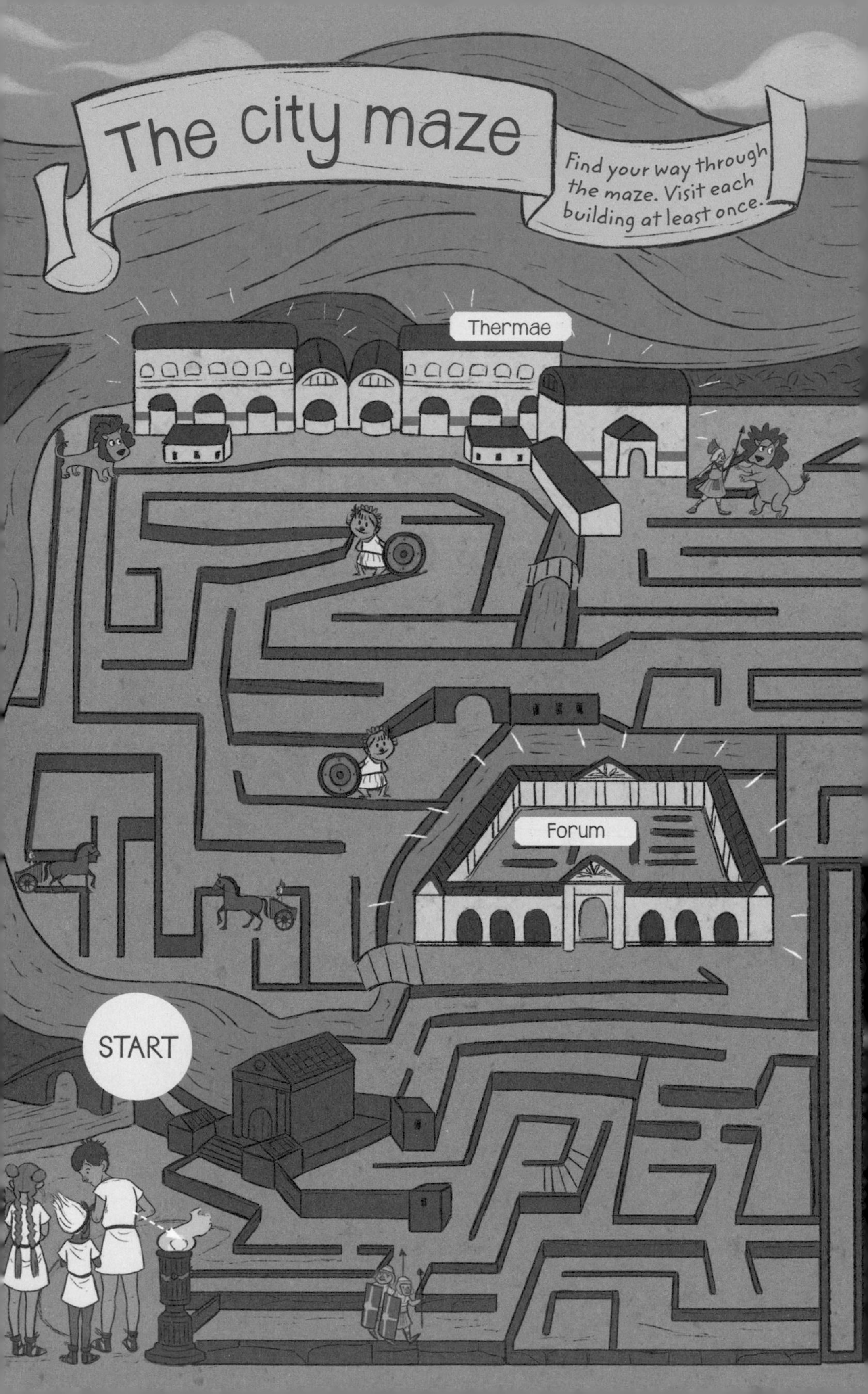
The city maze
Find your way through the maze. Visit each building at least once.
Thermae
Forum
START

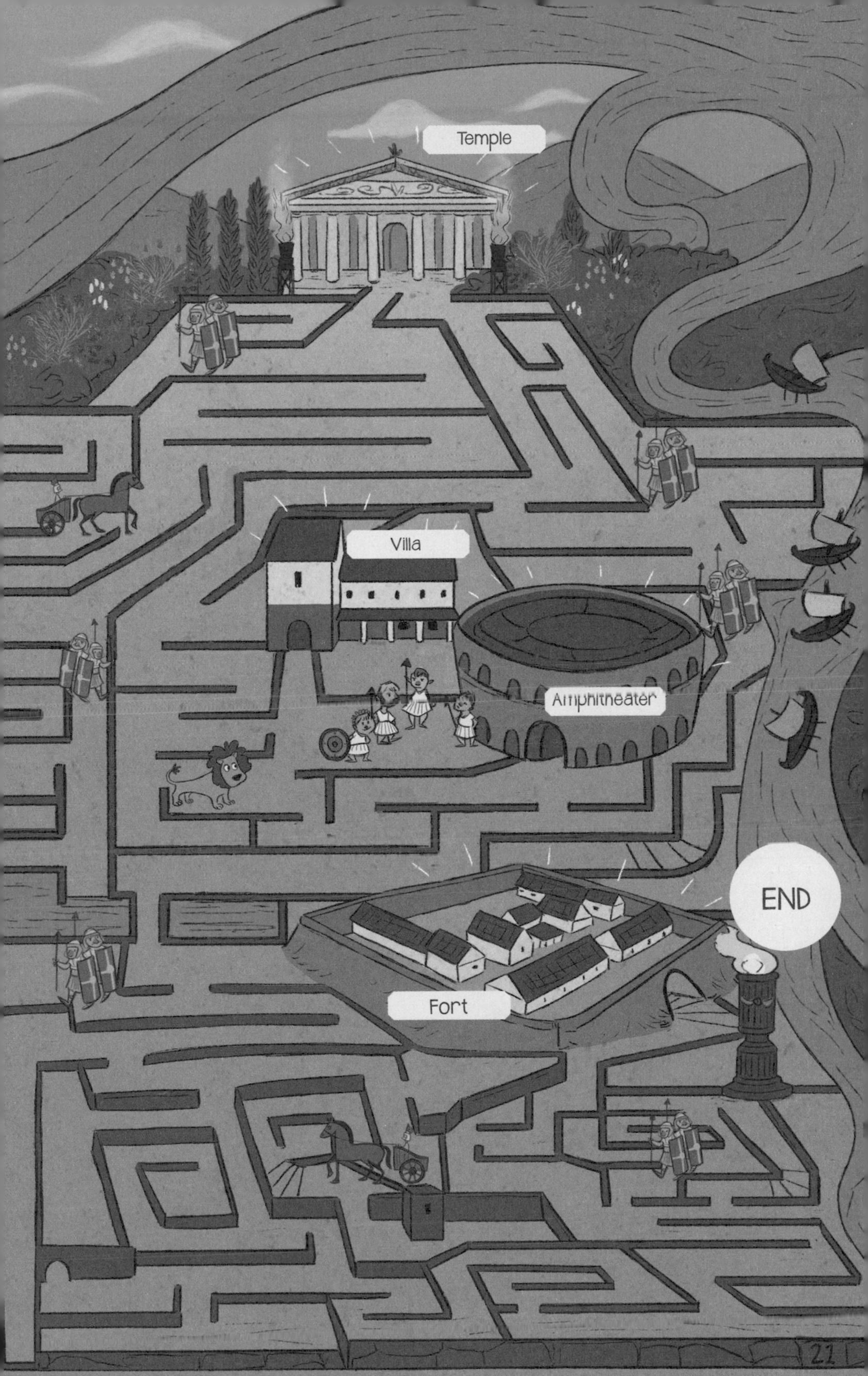
Temple
Villa
Amphitheater
END
Fort

Markets, money, and merels in ancient Rome

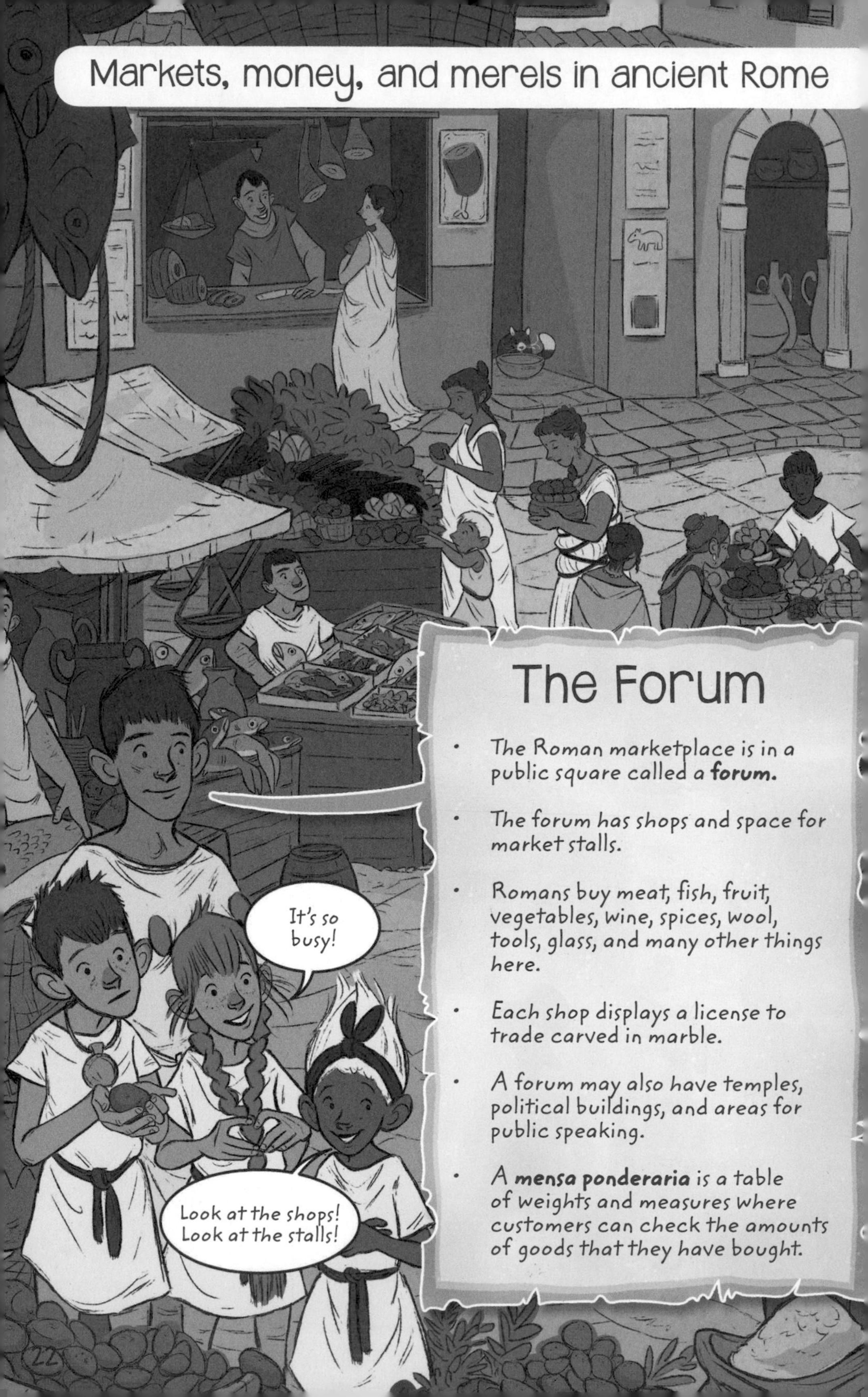
It's so busy!
Look at the shops! Look at the stalls!

The Forum

- The Roman marketplace is in a public square called a **forum.**
- The forum has shops and space for market stalls.
- Romans buy meat, fish, fruit, vegetables, wine, spices, wool, tools, glass, and many other things here.
- Each shop displays a license to trade carved in marble.
- A forum may also have temples, political buildings, and areas for public speaking.
- A **mensa ponderaria** is a table of weights and measures where customers can check the amounts of goods that they have bought.

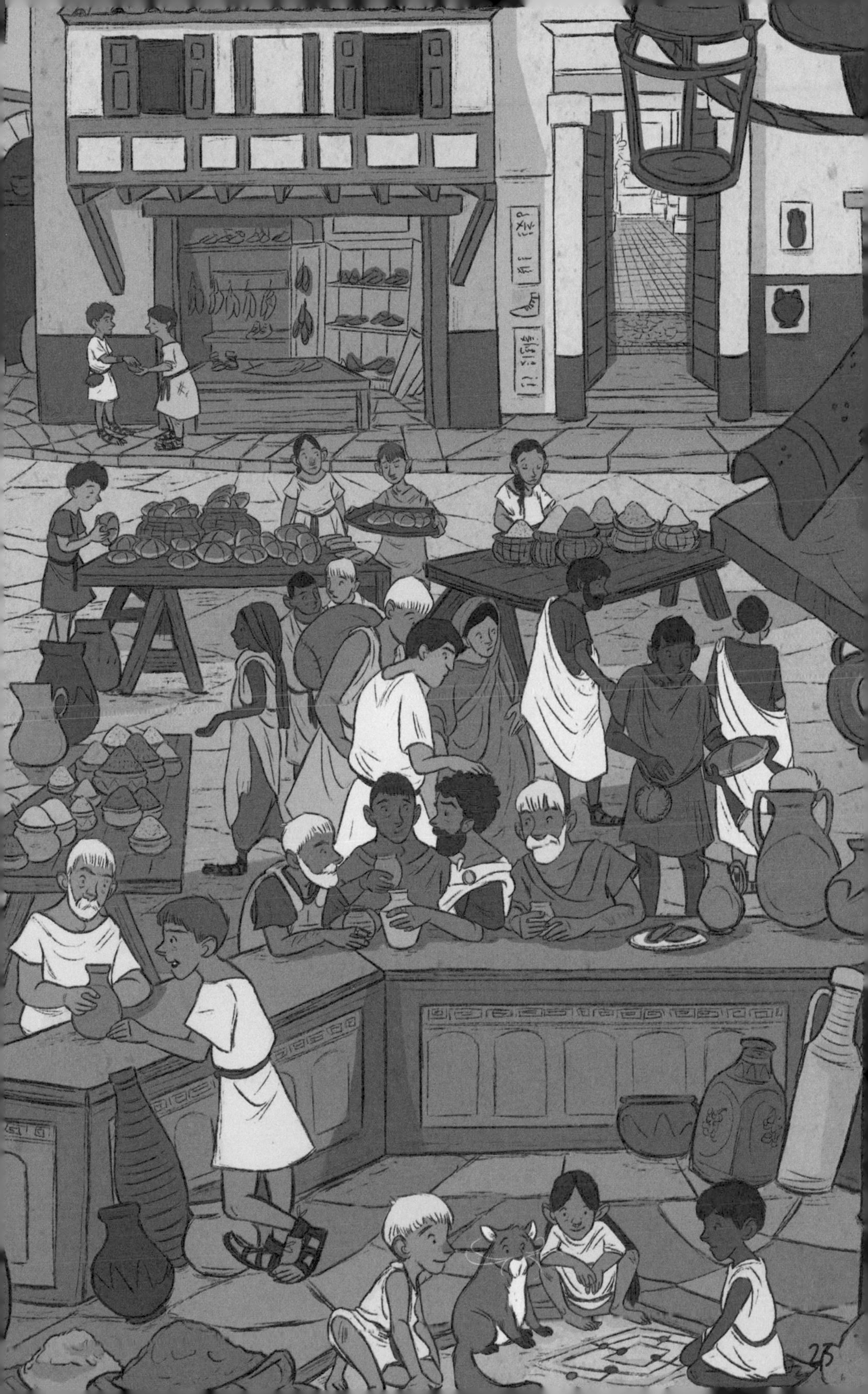

Latin words

The Romans speak and write in a language called Latin. Many Latin words have developed into words that appear in modern English today. Here are some examples.

canis
dog

modern word

canine

urbs
city

modern word

urban

ignis
fire

modern word

ignite

liber
book

modern word

library

mater
mother

modern words

**maternal,
maternity**

navis
ship

modern words

navy, naval

equus
horse

modern word

equestrian

manus
hand

modern word

manual

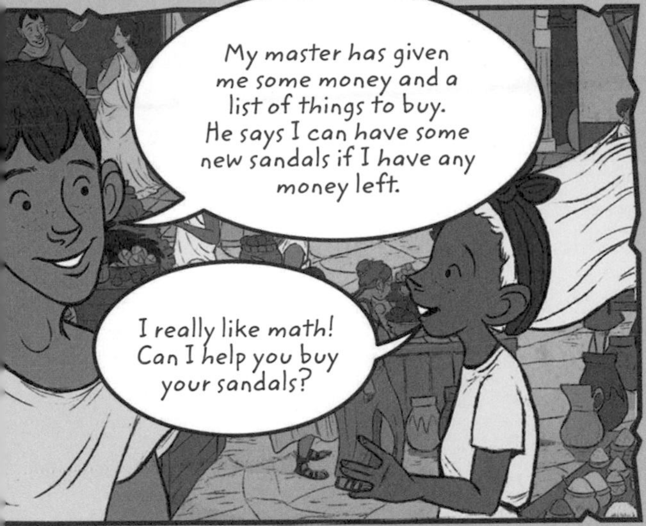
My master has given me some money and a list of things to buy. He says I can have some new sandals if I have any money left.
I really like math! Can I help you buy your sandals?

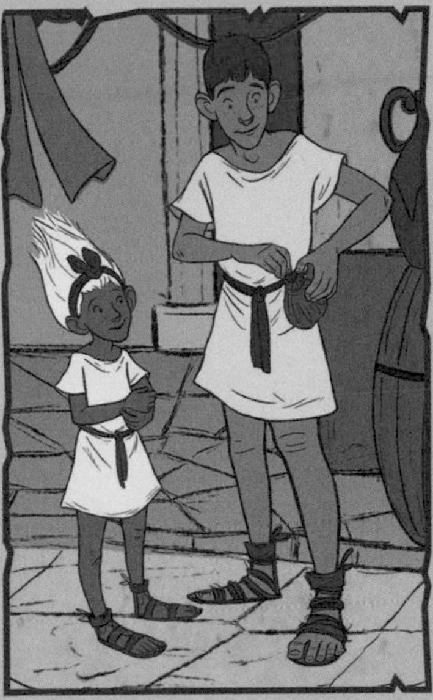

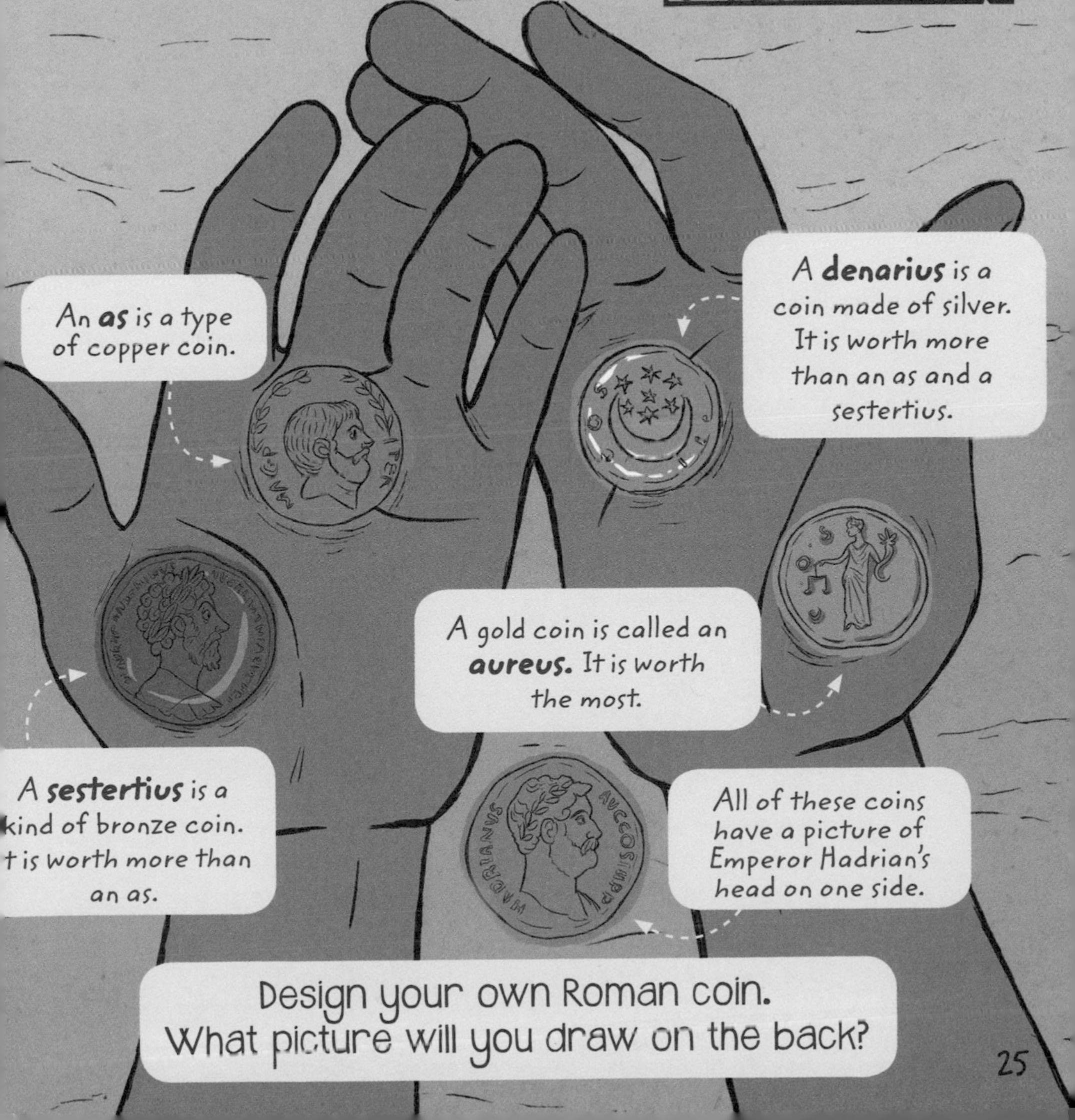
An **as** is a type of copper coin.
A **denarius** is a coin made of silver. It is worth more than an as and a sestertius.
A gold coin is called an **aureus.** It is worth the most.
A **sestertius** is a kind of bronze coin. It is worth more than an as.
All of these coins have a picture of Emperor Hadrian's head on one side.
Design your own Roman coin. What picture will you draw on the back?

Roman numerals

The Romans used seven different letters to count: **I, V, X, L, C, D,** and **M.**

1 = **I**	20 = **XX**	
2 = **II**	30 = **XXX**	100 = **C**
3 = **III**	40 = **XL**	
4 = **IV**	50 = **L**	500 = **D**
5 = **V**	60 = **LX**	
6 = **VI**	70 = **LXX**	1000 = **M**
7 = **VII**	80 = **LXXX**	
8 = **VIII**	90 = **XC**	2000 = **MM**
9 = **IX**		
10 = **X**		

Roman numerals are tricky. To understand all of the numbers, it is useful to know the numbers 1 to 9 first. For bigger numbers, add the numerals together.

$$\textbf{XV} \text{ is } \underline{10 + 5 = 15}$$

The bigger numbers usually come first. But there are some traps! If a low number comes before a high number, it is subtracted. For example, the numbers 14 and 16 contain the same numerals as each other but in a different order:

$$\textbf{XIV} \text{ is } \underline{14} \quad \text{and} \quad \textbf{XVI} \text{ is } \underline{16}$$

Work out what these numbers are.

LVIII	XVIII
XXVI	DVI
VIII	XLV
CCIV	MLIII

Turn our numbers into Roman ones.

22	520
67	109
5	99
18	52

Try some addition.

X + IV = ?
L + III = ?
M + L + X = ?
D + IV = ?
C + XXVI = ?

Try some subtraction.

X − II = ?
D − LX = ?
V − I = ?
C − XXII = ?
CC − LXXXI = ?

Nani has **25 denarii.** Can Messenio buy his new sandals?

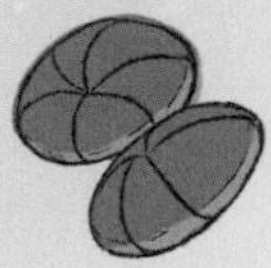

two loaves of bread = **III denarii**

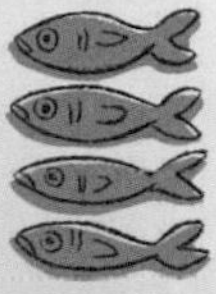

four whole fish = **V denarii**

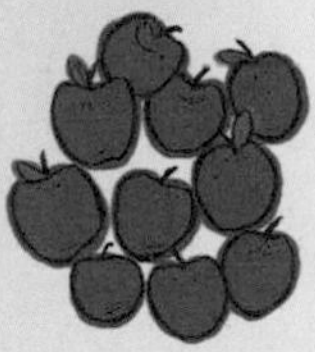

ten apples = **II denarii**

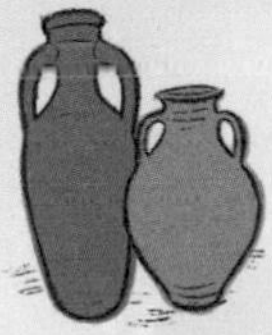

two amphorae of wine = **VI denarii**

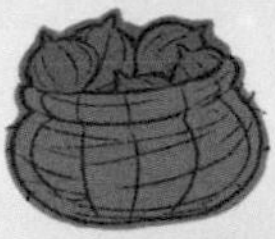

a basket of figs = **IV denarii**

Is there enough left for Messenio's new sandals?

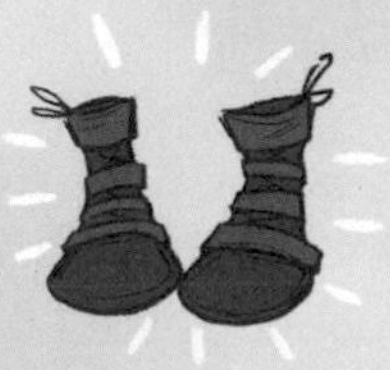

a pair of new sandals = **V denarii**

Look at Hero — he's found a game!

Play **merels** with us!

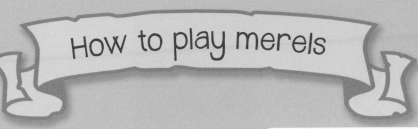

How to play merels

What to do:

Players: two

Each player starts with 10 counters of one color. The aim of the game is to take turns to put a counter on one of the spots. The winner is the first person to get three counters in a row in any direction.

You will need:

- 10 counters of one color and 10 counters of another color

Merels board drawn in the sand

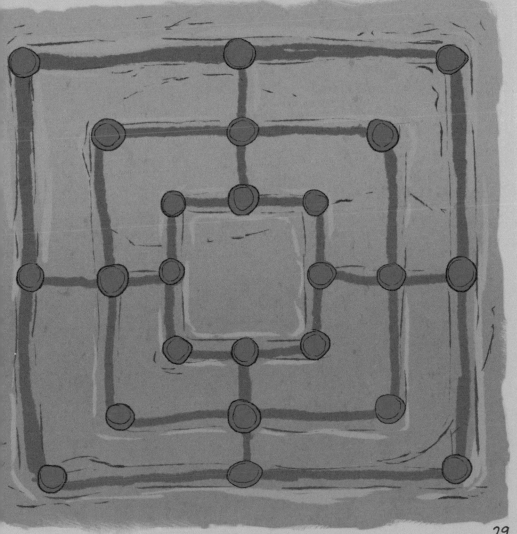

29

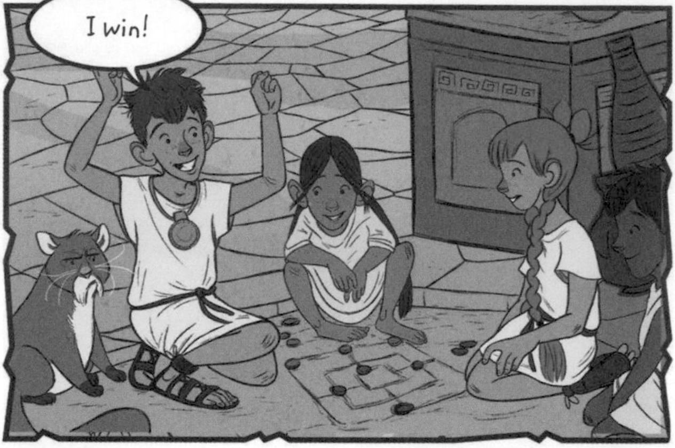
I win!

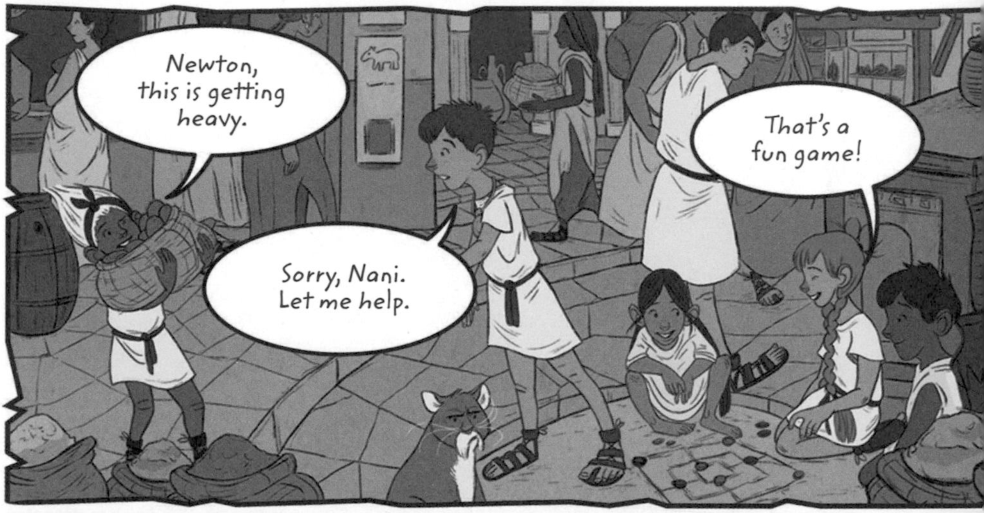
Newton, this is getting heavy.
Sorry, Nani. Let me help.
That's a fun game!

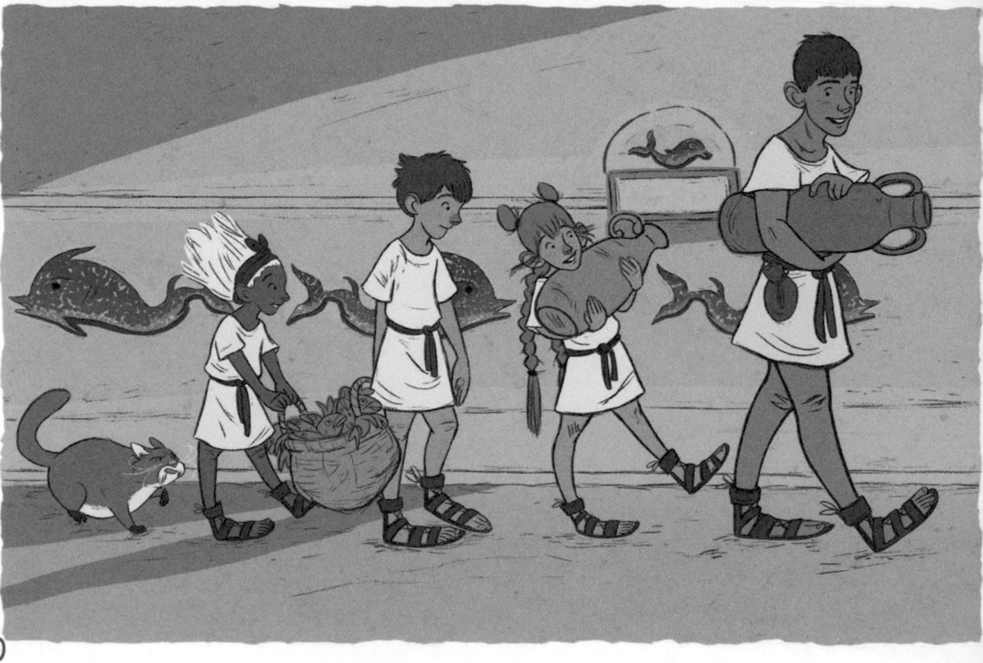

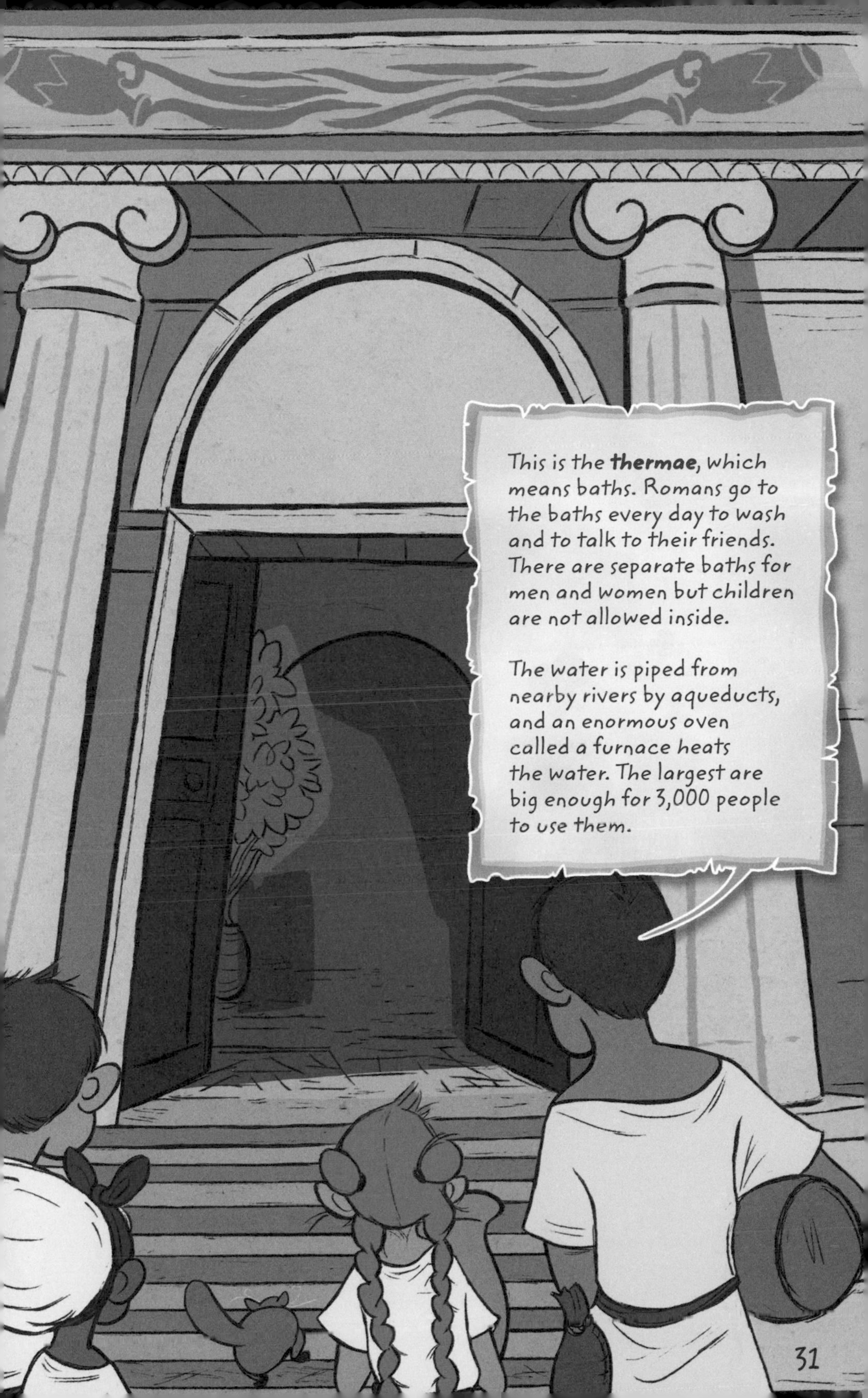
This is the **thermae**, which means baths. Romans go to the baths every day to wash and to talk to their friends. There are separate baths for men and women but children are not allowed inside.
The water is piped from nearby rivers by aqueducts, and an enormous oven called a furnace heats the water. The largest are big enough for 3,000 people to use them.

Make a model aqueduct

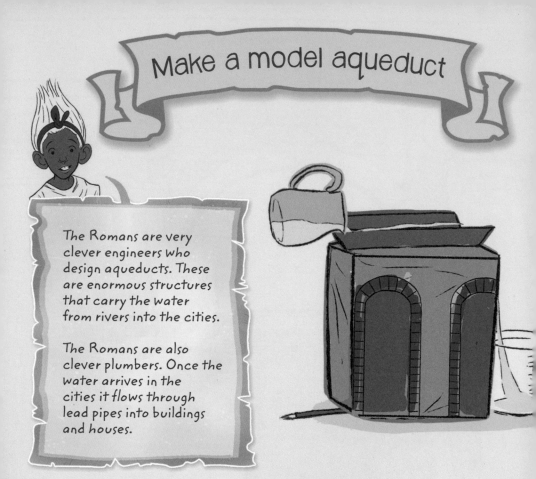

The Romans are very clever engineers who design aqueducts. These are enormous structures that carry the water from rivers into the cities.

The Romans are also clever plumbers. Once the water arrives in the cities it flows through lead pipes into buildings and houses.

You will need:

- An empty cereal box
- Scissors
- Glue
- Cardstock
- Paper
- A pencil
- Colored pencils
- A beaker
- A jug of water

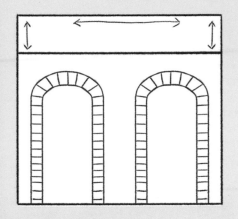

1. Cut two pieces of paper the same size as the cereal box, including the flaps at the top, and copy this image onto them.

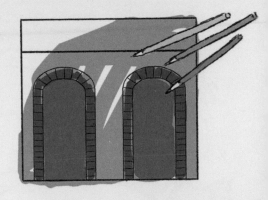

2. Color the image!

3. Glue the pictures onto the outside of the cereal box and onto the flaps at the top.

4. Fold over the flaps at the top and glue them together.

5. Cut three lengths of thin cardstock to make a channel for the viaduct. Glue one strip to the top of the box. Fold the other two in half lengthwise. Place these two back-to-back on top of the box so they make a V shape together. Glue them in place. Cover them in glue and leave them to dry.

6. Place a pencil under one end of the box to create a slope. Put a beaker at the other end. Pour water into the channel at the higher end and it will run into the beaker.

Hero takes a Roman bath

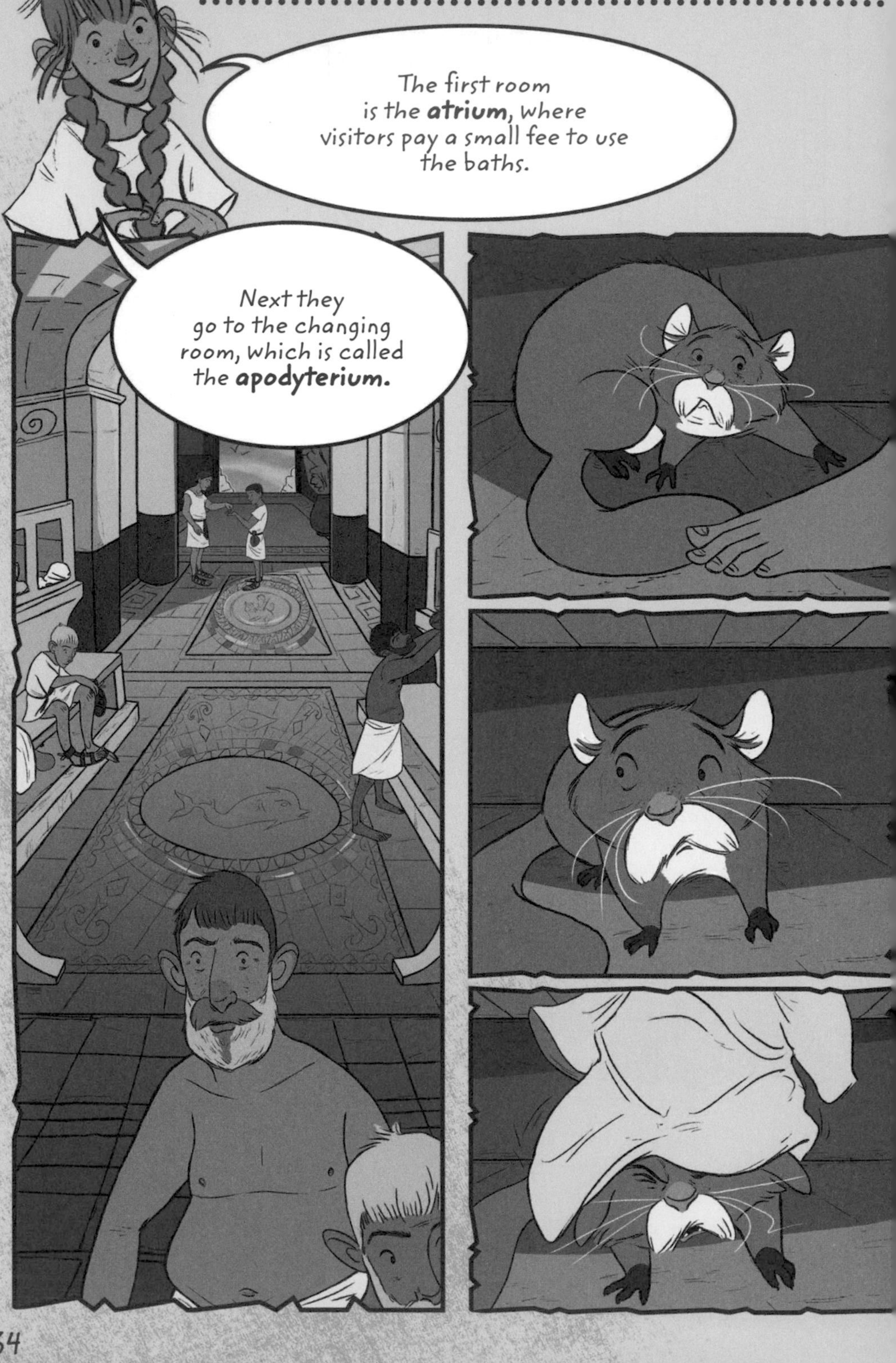

The first room is the **atrium**, where visitors pay a small fee to use the baths.
Next they go to the changing room, which is called the **apodyterium.**

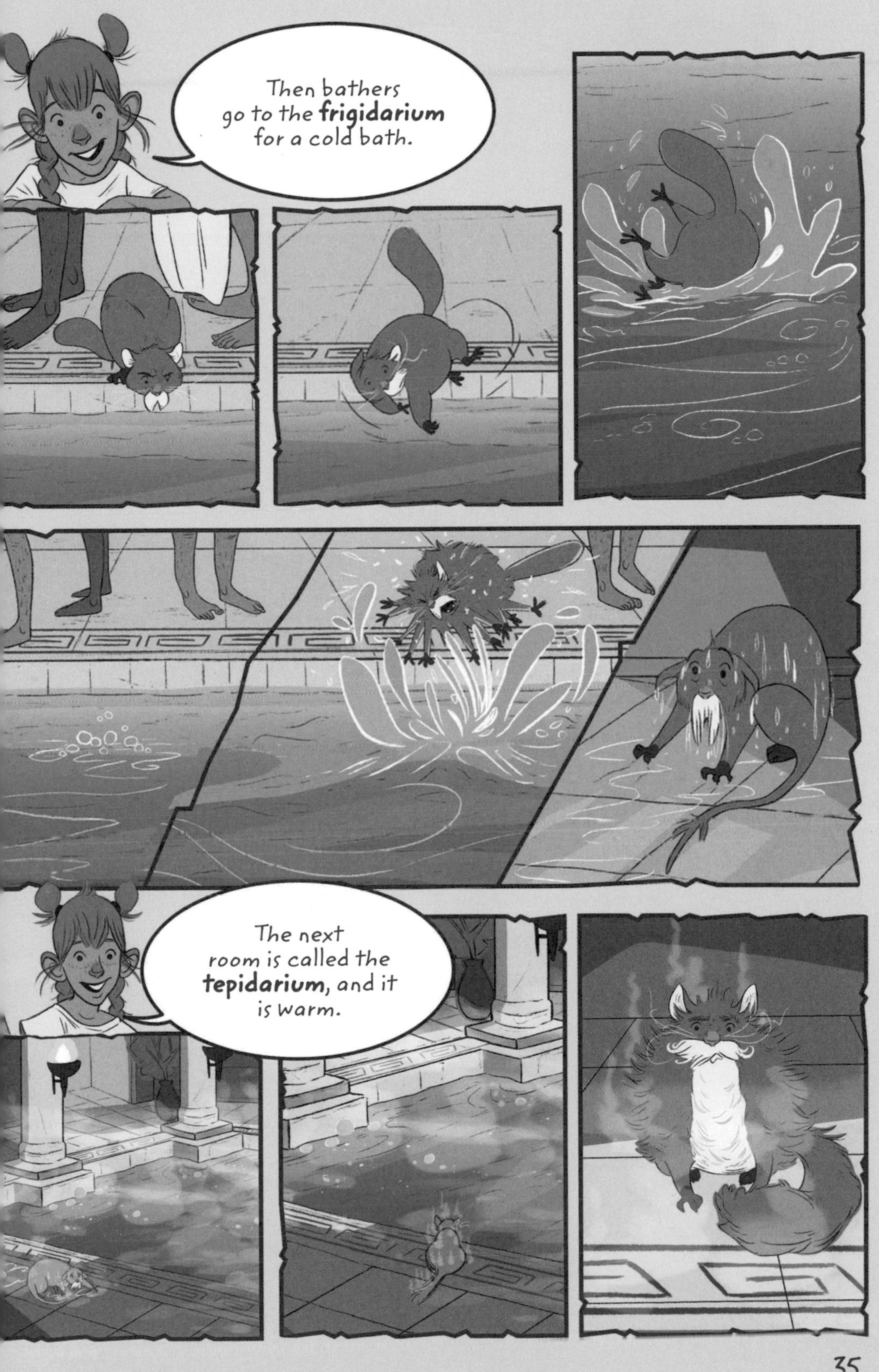
Then bathers go to the **frigidarium** for a cold bath.
The next room is called the **tepidarium**, and it is warm.

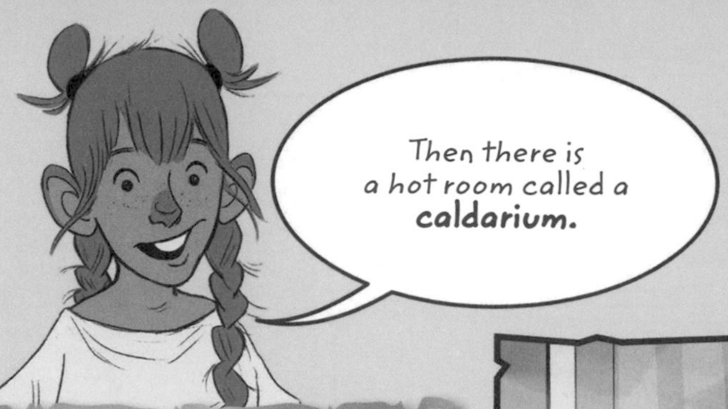
Then there is a hot room called a **caldarium.**

How it works

- Romans use the furnace to push hot air into spaces under the floor and in the walls.
- This heating system is called a ***hypocaust***.
- Soap is very expensive so bathers remove dirt by covering themselves in oil and scraping it off with an object called a strigil.

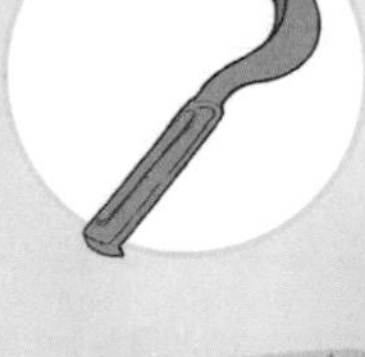

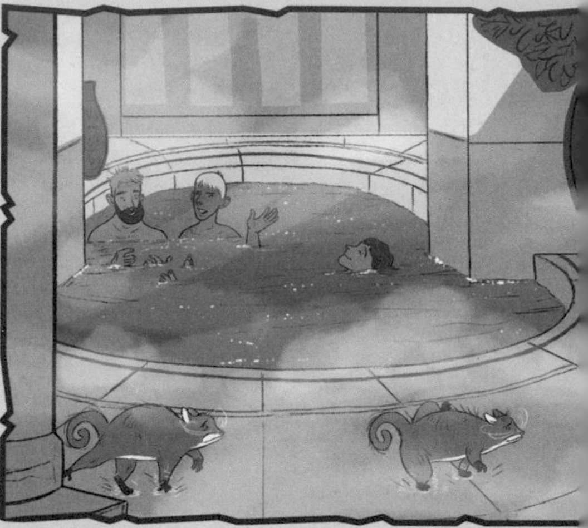

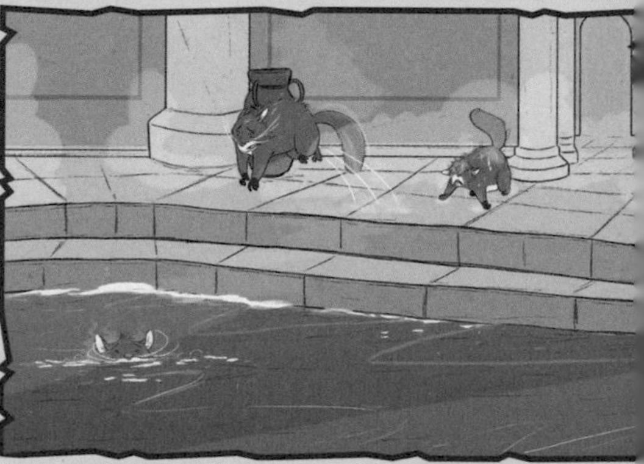

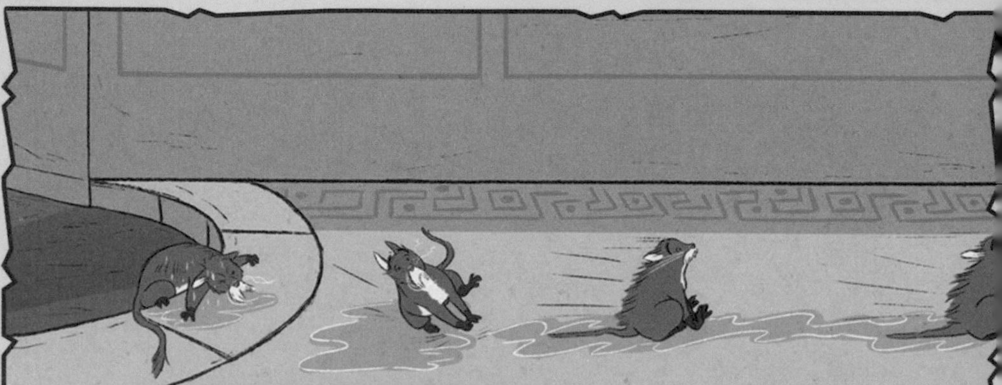

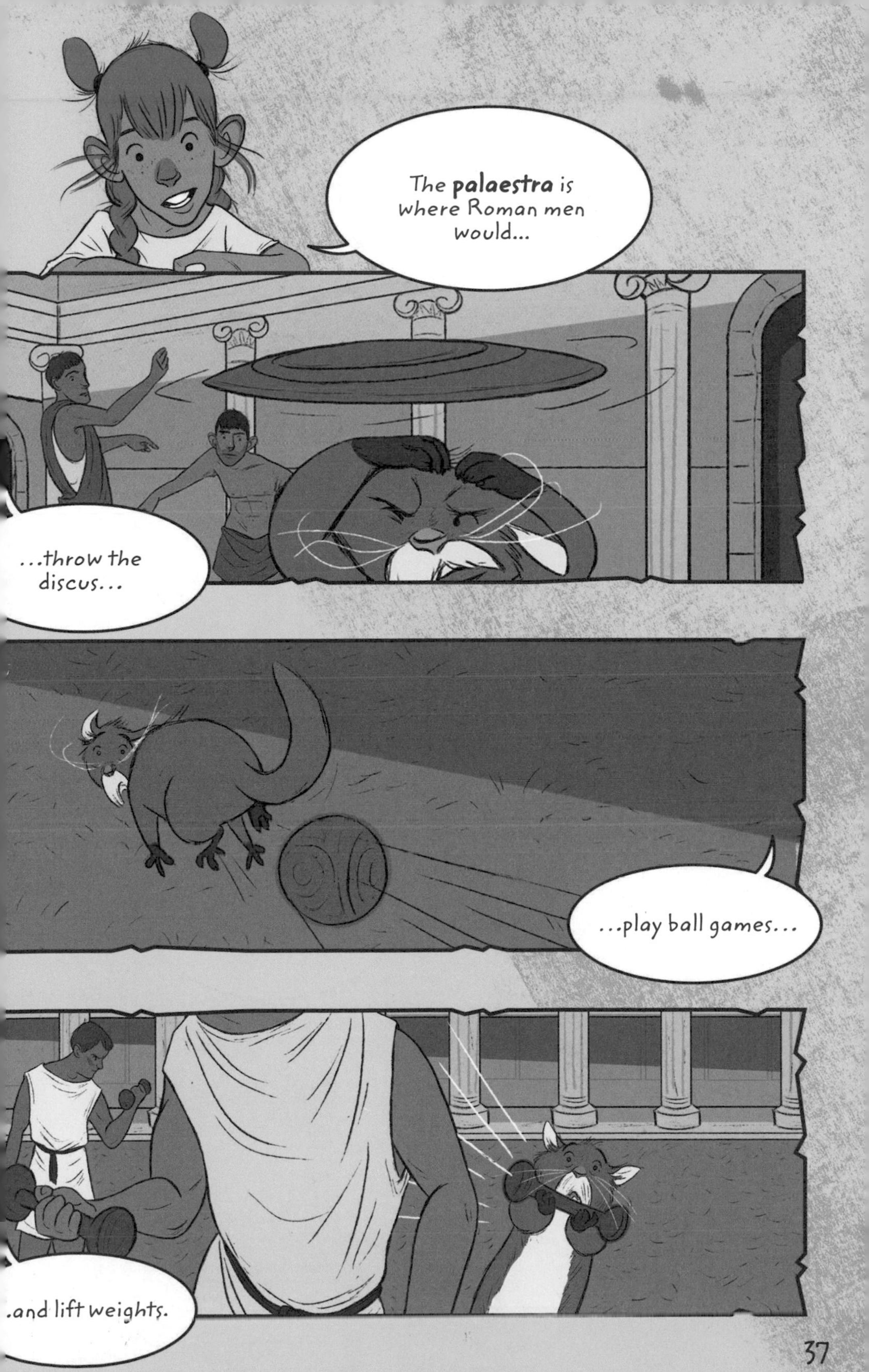

The **palaestra** is where Roman men would...
...throw the discus...
...play ball games...
.and lift weights.

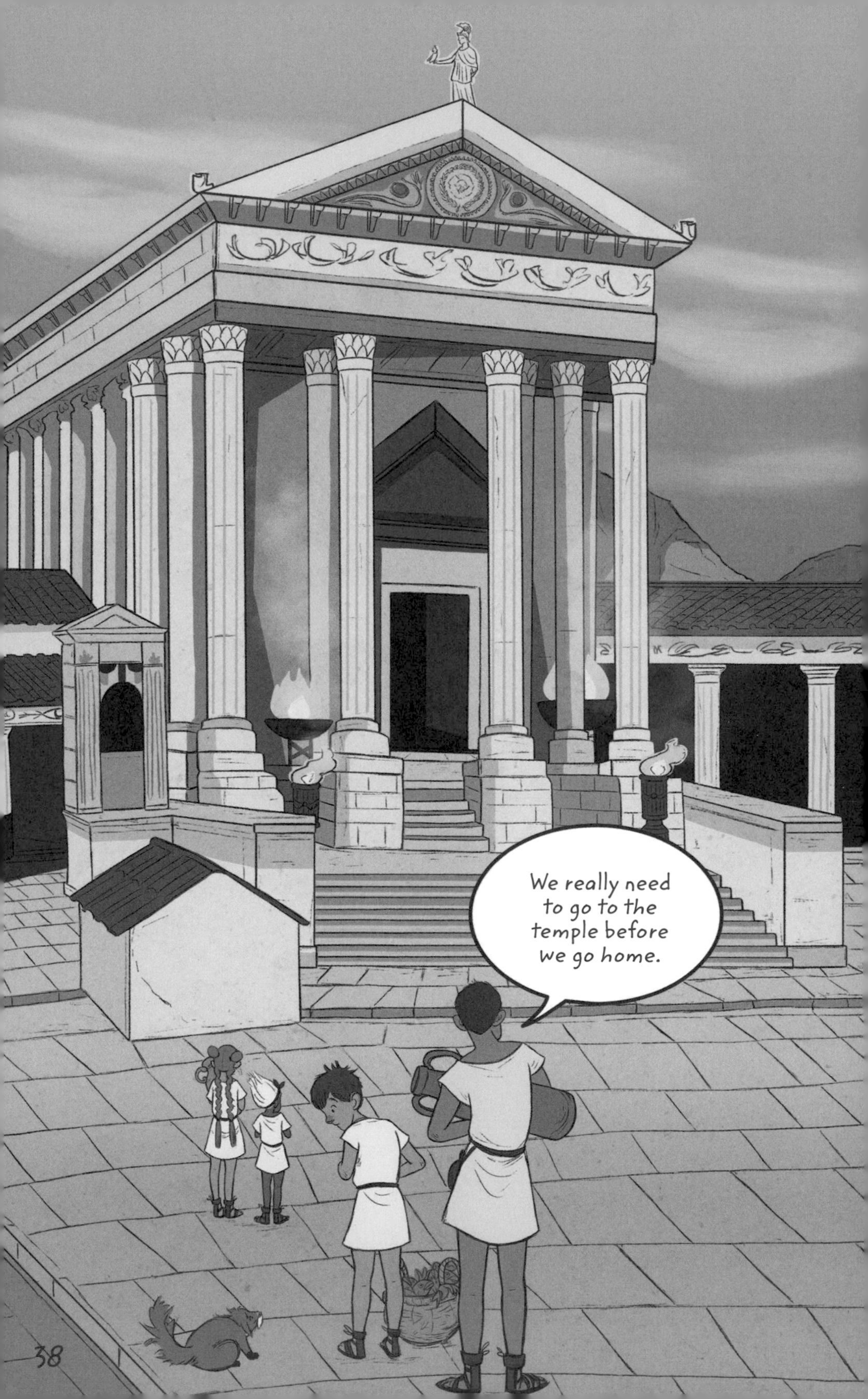
We really need to go to the temple before we go home.

Inside the Temple of Minerva

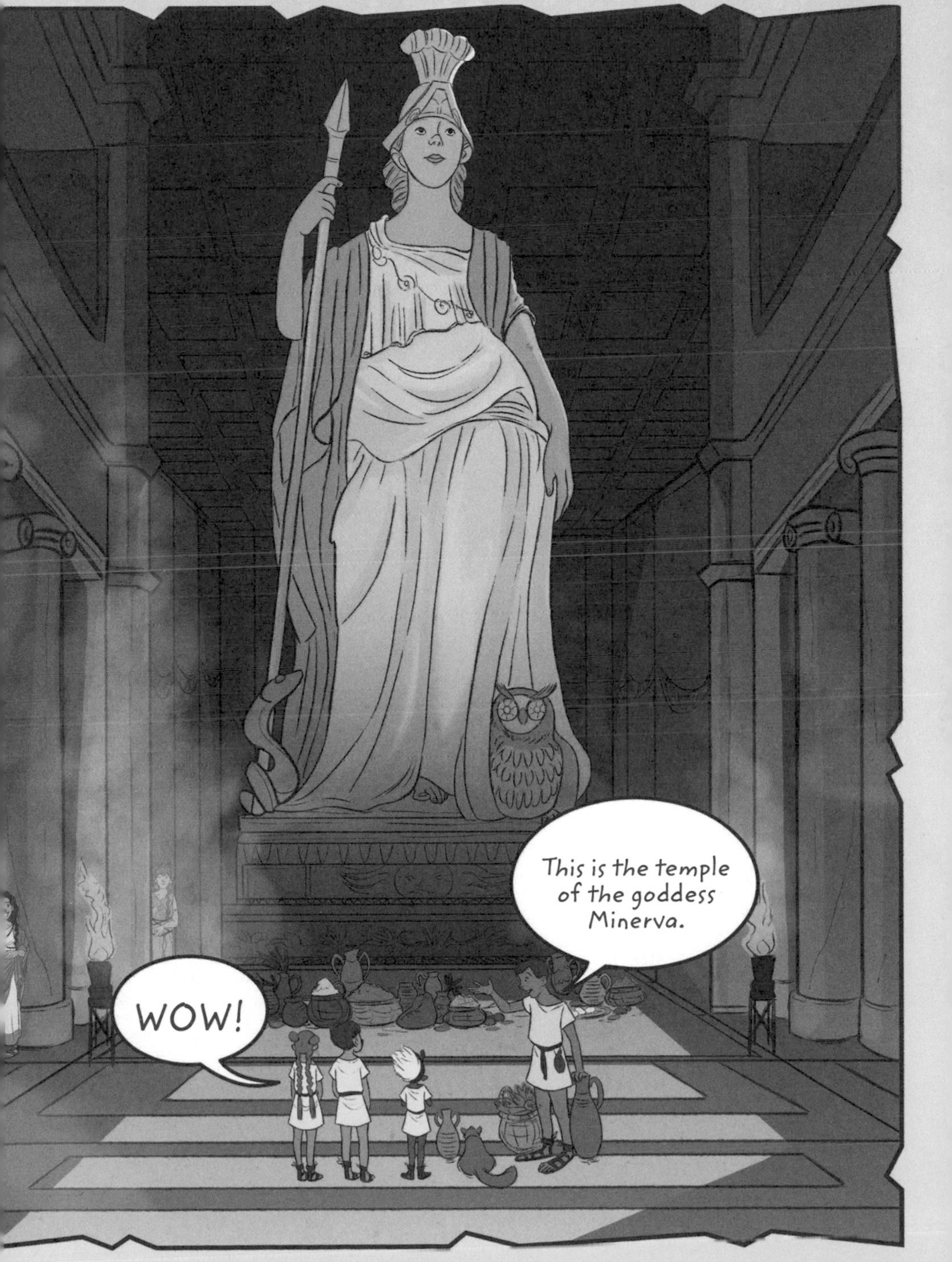
This is the temple of the goddess Minerva.
WOW!

Roman gods and goddesses

I know about some Roman gods!

Juno

Status: Queen of the Roman gods

Symbol: Peacock

"I am the sister of Jupiter, Pluto, and Neptune. The month of June gets its name from me, not the other way around. I protect marriage and childbirth."

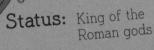

Jupiter

Status: King of the Roman gods

Symbol: Thunderbolt and eagle

"My father was called Saturn but I overthrew him and became ruler of the gods in his place. I am the most powerful of all the Roman gods! Minerva and Mars are my children."

Minerva

Status: Goddess of wisdom and medicine

Symbol: Owl, snake, and olive tree

"I was born from the head of my father, Jupiter, who is the king of the Roman gods."

Neptune

Status: Ruler of the seas!

Symbol: Trident

"I ride across the sea on dolphins or on a shell pulled by seahorses. Some people blame me for earthquakes."

Pluto

Status: God of the underworld

Symbol: Two-pronged, forklike staff and large key

"Jupiter and Neptune are my brothers. I have a dog called Cerberus—he has three heads. Also, I have a helmet that can make me invisible."

Venus

Status: Goddess of love

Symbol: Scallop shell, dove, and pearls

"I was born from sea-foam and floated to shore on a shell."

Diana

Status: Goddess of hunting

Symbol: Moon, bow, and arrow

"My twin brother is Apollo. I am the protector of women."

Mars

Status: God of war

Symbol: Spear and vulture

"I am the son of Jupiter and Juno. The month of March gets its name from me."

Apollo

Status: God of the sun and music

Symbol: Sun and lyre

"My twin sister is Diana."

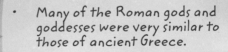

- Many of the Roman gods and goddesses were very similar to those of ancient Greece.

- The Romans are famous for taking bits from other cultures.

- They often kept the gods of the people that they conquered but sometimes gave them new names.

- This meant that when the Romans took over a new piece of land, the people already living there could carry on worshipping their own gods and goddesses.

Gifts for the gods

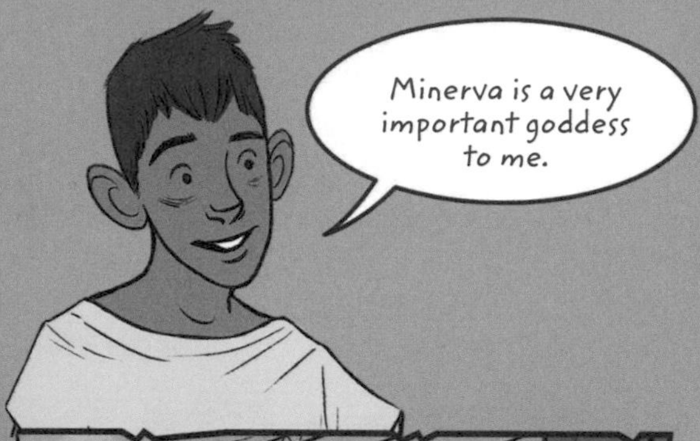
Minerva is a very important goddess to me.

Making an offering

- Romans give offerings to their gods and goddesses as thanks or to ask for good fortune.
- A simple type of offering is called a libation.
- A libation involves a worshipper pouring a little bit of wine, milk, oil, or honey onto the ground or an altar as a gift to the gods.
- Throwing breadcrumbs into a fire or sacrificing an animal in the name of a god are other kinds of offering.

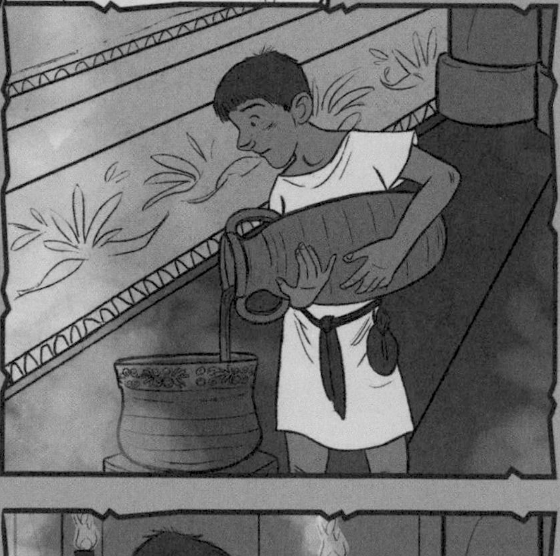

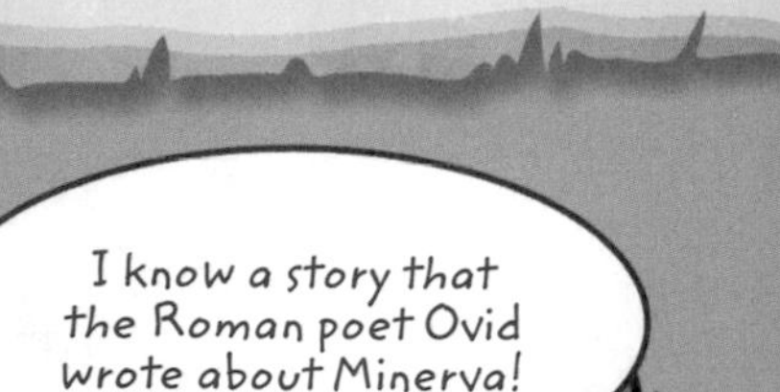

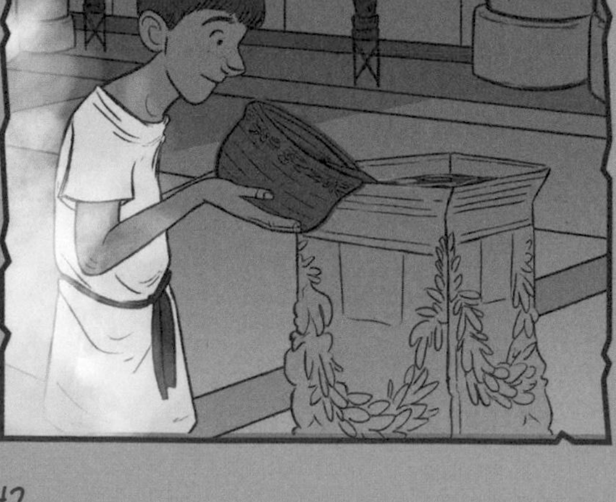

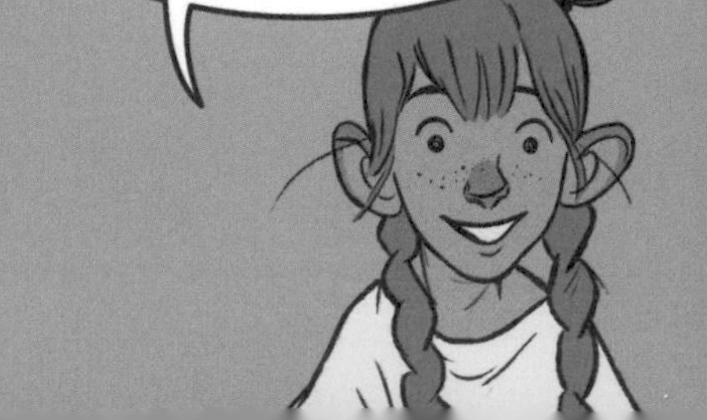
I know a story that the Roman poet Ovid wrote about Minerva!

There was once a child named Arachne. Her father was a shepherd and they were very poor so Arachne learned to weave on a loom to earn some money. She became a wonderful weaver who created the most beautiful tapestries.

The news of her skill spread far and wide. She became very famous and also very proud. People told her that she was so good that the goddess Minerva had to be helping her in her work. Now, Arachne did not like to hear that people thought she had help from a god. She told the people that she worked on her own and that she was the greatest weaver. One day, as she worked at her loom, an old woman came to visit her.

The woman told the girl that she must never claim to be more skilled than any of the gods as they would punish her for being so proud. But if she prayed to Minerva, she might forgive her for boasting.

Arachne laughed at the woman and said that the goddess should come and challenge her in person. Then they would see who was the better weaver. As she spoke the old woman removed her disguise and showed the girl that she really was Minerva herself. The goddess challenged Arachne to a contest and so the two began to weave. Minerva wove a tapestry which showed the gods punishing mortals for their pride and for claiming to be equal to the gods. Arachne's picture showed how the gods could be cruel and unforgiving.

When they had finished, Arachne's picture was not only insulting to Minerva, but it was also far more beautiful than her own. Minerva was so angry that she punished Arachne by turning her into a spider who would be forced to weave forever!

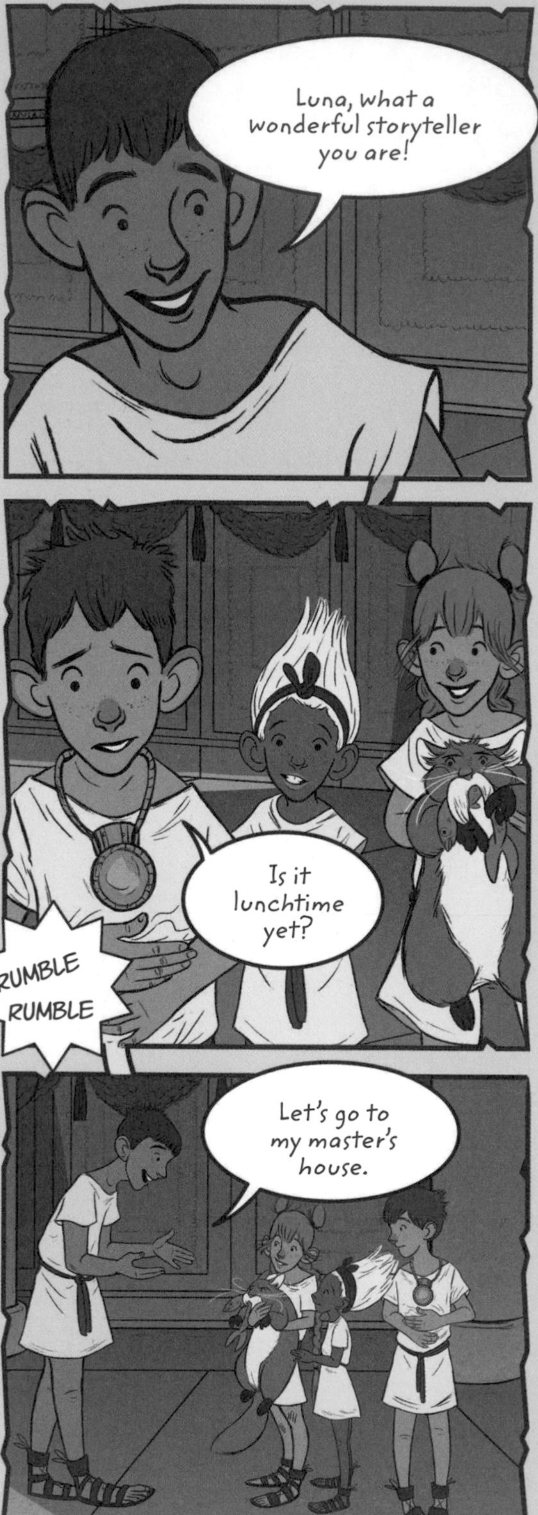
Luna, what a wonderful storyteller you are!
Is it lunchtime yet?
RUMBLE RUMBLE
Let's go to my master's house.

Houses and homes

- Roman houses can be lots of different shapes and sizes.
- Some small houses have shops in them so that their owners can work at home and sell their goods.
- A large Roman house is called a **villa** and rich people live in them.
- Lead pipes bring running water into these large houses, some of which even have underfloor heating.

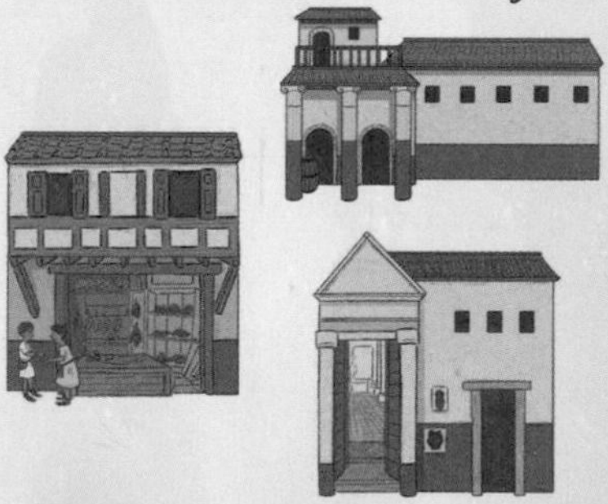

- Paintings and mosaics make a villa look nice.

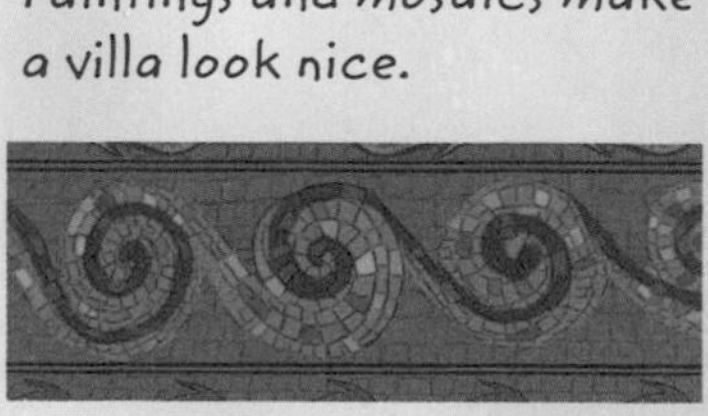

There's no place like a Roman home

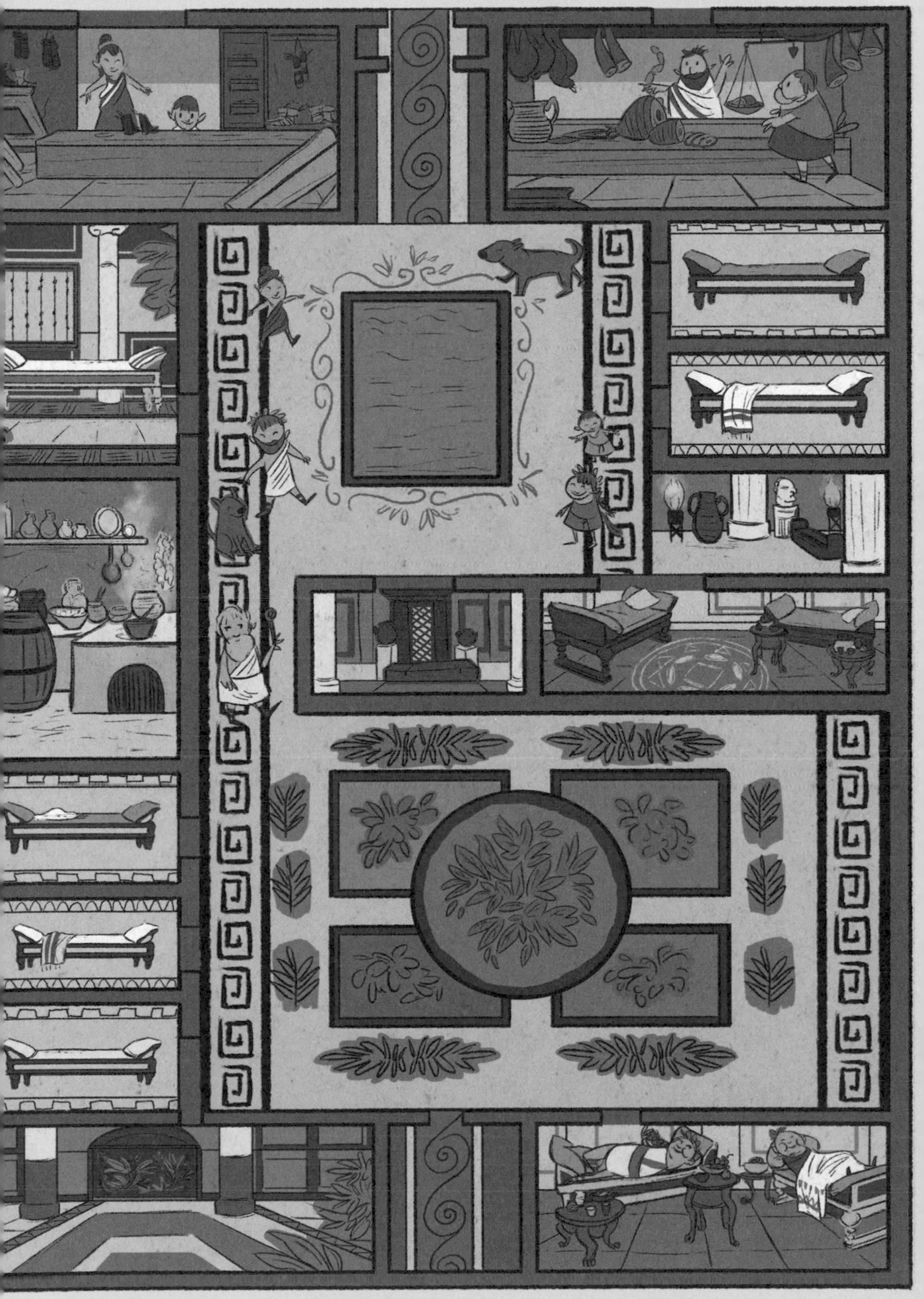

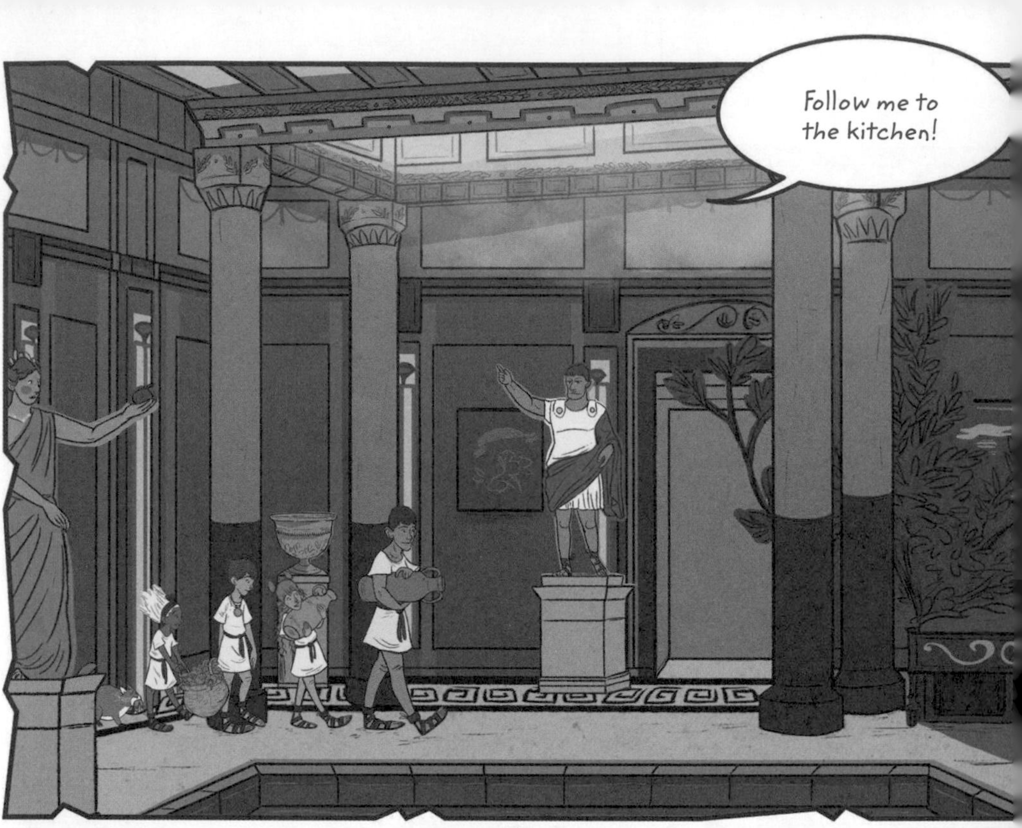
Follow me to the kitchen!

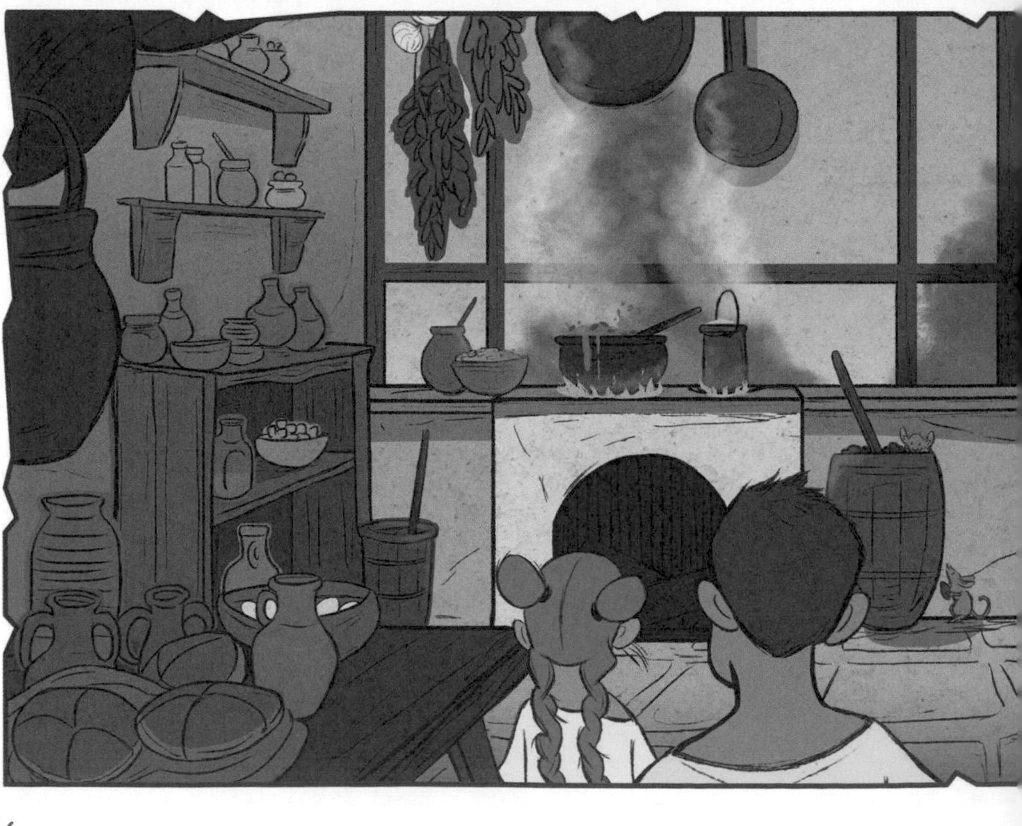

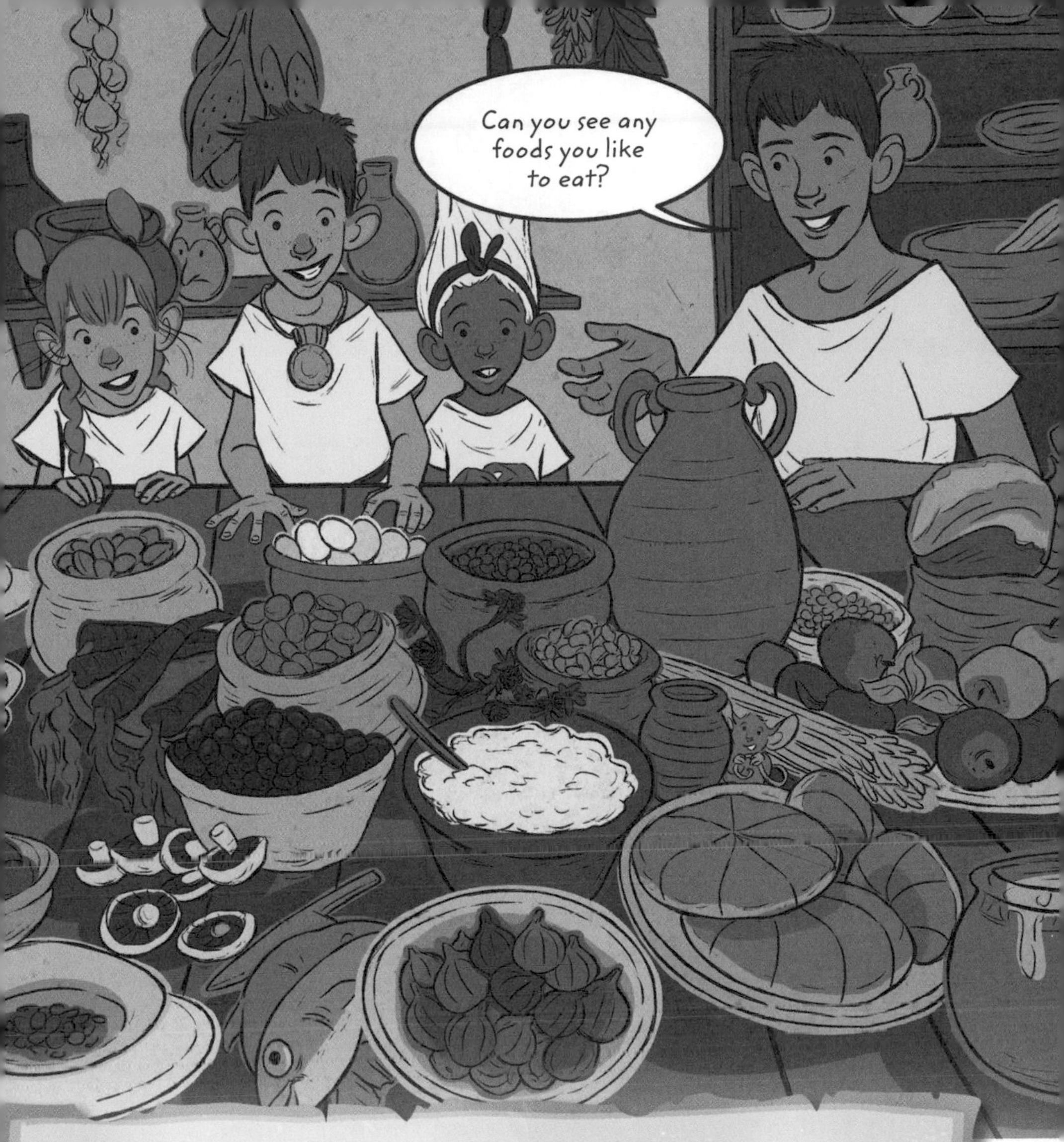
Can you see any foods you like to eat?

Roman meals

- The Romans eat lots of foods that are still familiar today, for example fruit and vegetables and meat.
- There are also foods which are probably not so common today, like dormice (mice found in Europe) and peacocks.
- They don't have sugar so they use honey to sweeten their food.
- They drink fruit juices, beer, and wine.
- They call breakfast **ientaculum**.
- Lunch is called **prandium**.
- Dinner is called **cena**.

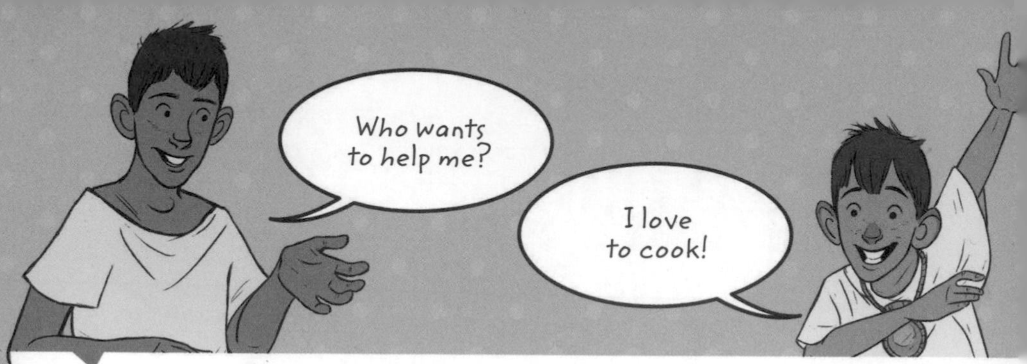
Who wants to help me?
I love to cook!

Recipe for Roman honey cakes

Always wash your hands before cooking and make sure you get an adult to help you use the oven.

Ingredients:
1/3 cup (50g) flour (spelt flour is most similar to the flour the Romans used but plain flour is fine instead, white or brown)
3 eggs
scant 2/3 cup (200g) liquid honey

Preheat the oven to 325°F (170°C).
Grease a baking tin.
Beat the eggs together until they have lots of air bubbles and are stiff.
Mix in the honey.
Gently fold in the flour and mix everything together.
Pour the mix into the baking tin.
Put into the oven for 50 minutes.
After it has baked, turn the cake out onto a wire rack to cool.

Enjoy!

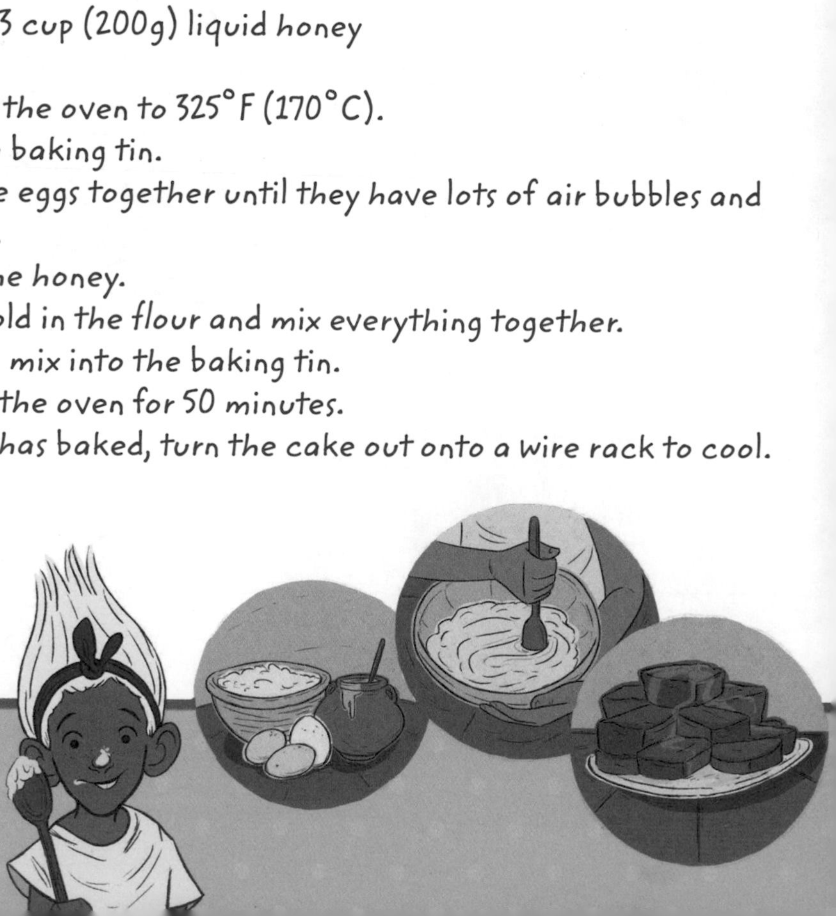

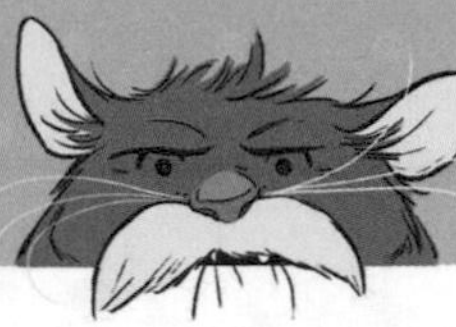

Recipe for Roman "aliter dulcia" ("another dessert")

Always wash your hands before cooking and make sure you get an adult to help you use the oven.

Ingredients:
4 slices of white bread with the crusts cut off
scant 3 1/4 cup (75 ml) milk
1 egg
2 tablespoons honey plus more for topping
Oil

Break the bread into large pieces.
Beat the eggs and mix them with the milk.
Put the bread into the milk and honey mix so it soaks the liquid up.
Heat some oil in a frying pan.
Fry the bread in the pan.
When it is cooked, cover it with even more honey and enjoy!

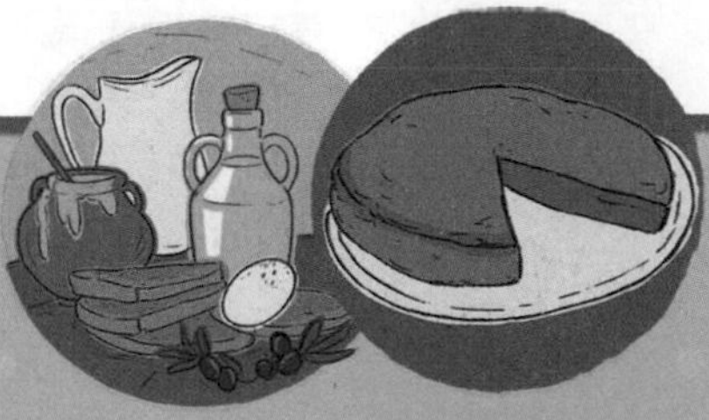

At the table

Wealthy Romans do not sit at tables to eat but they do eat in a formal dining room called a **triclinium**.
They eat lying down on couches called **klinai**, and three of these klinai would be arranged around a low table. Slaves bring food to the diners and musicians play while they eat.

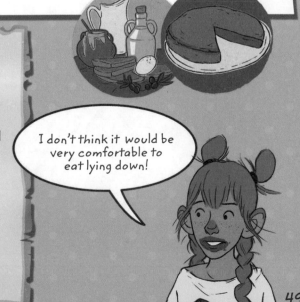

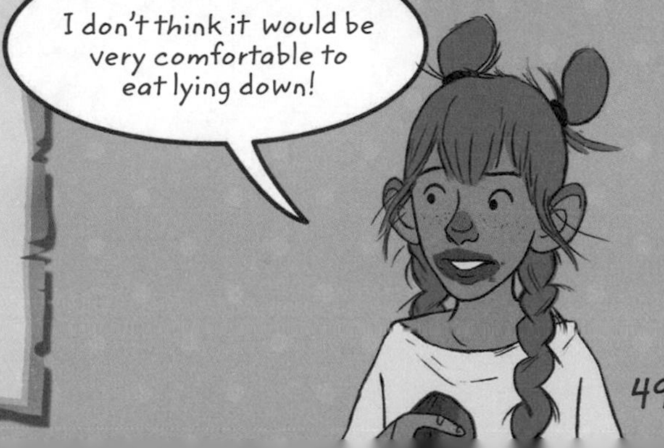
I don't think it would be very comfortable to eat lying down!

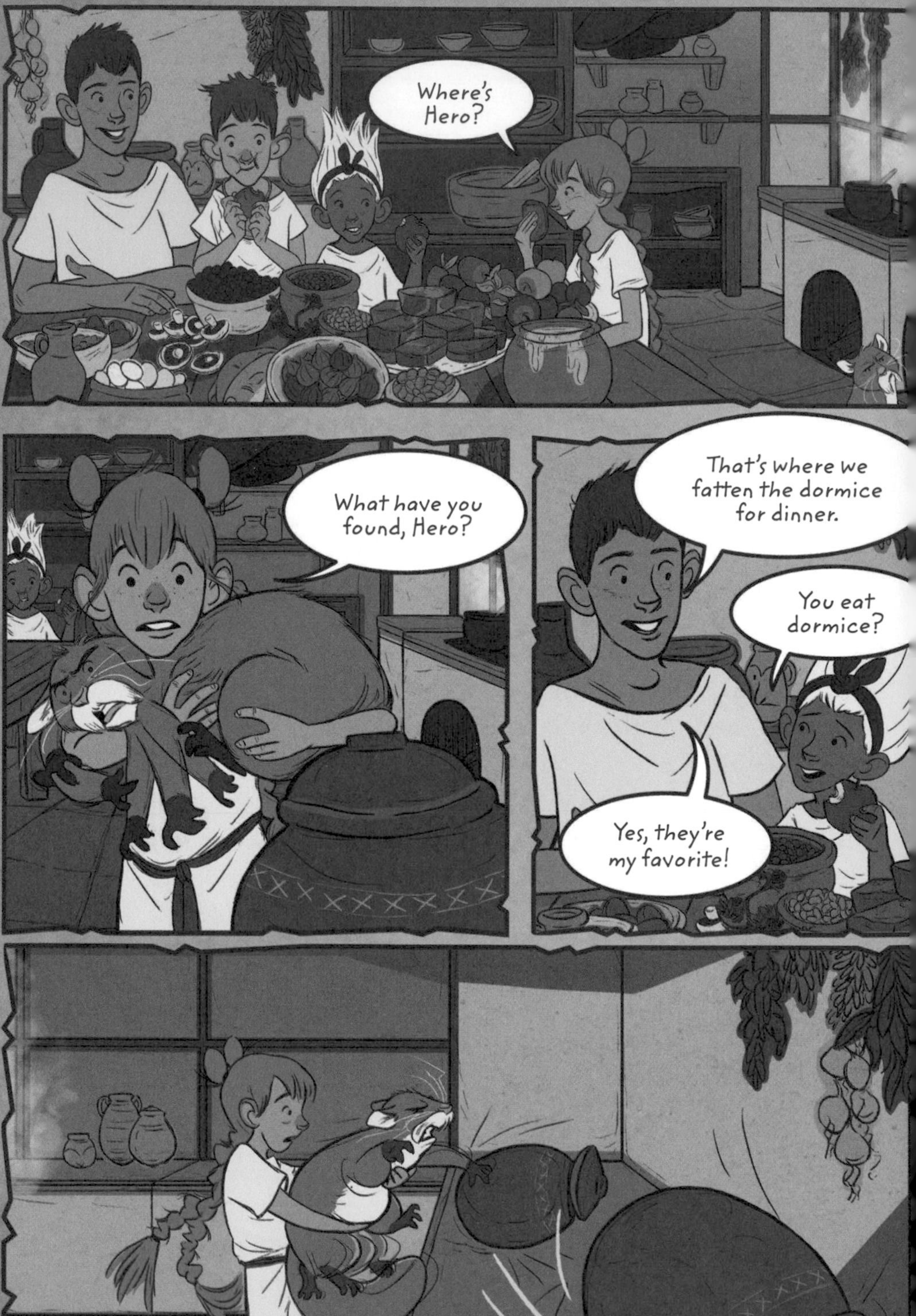
Where's Hero?
What have you found, Hero?
That's where we fatten the dormice for dinner.
You eat dormice?
Yes, they're my favorite!

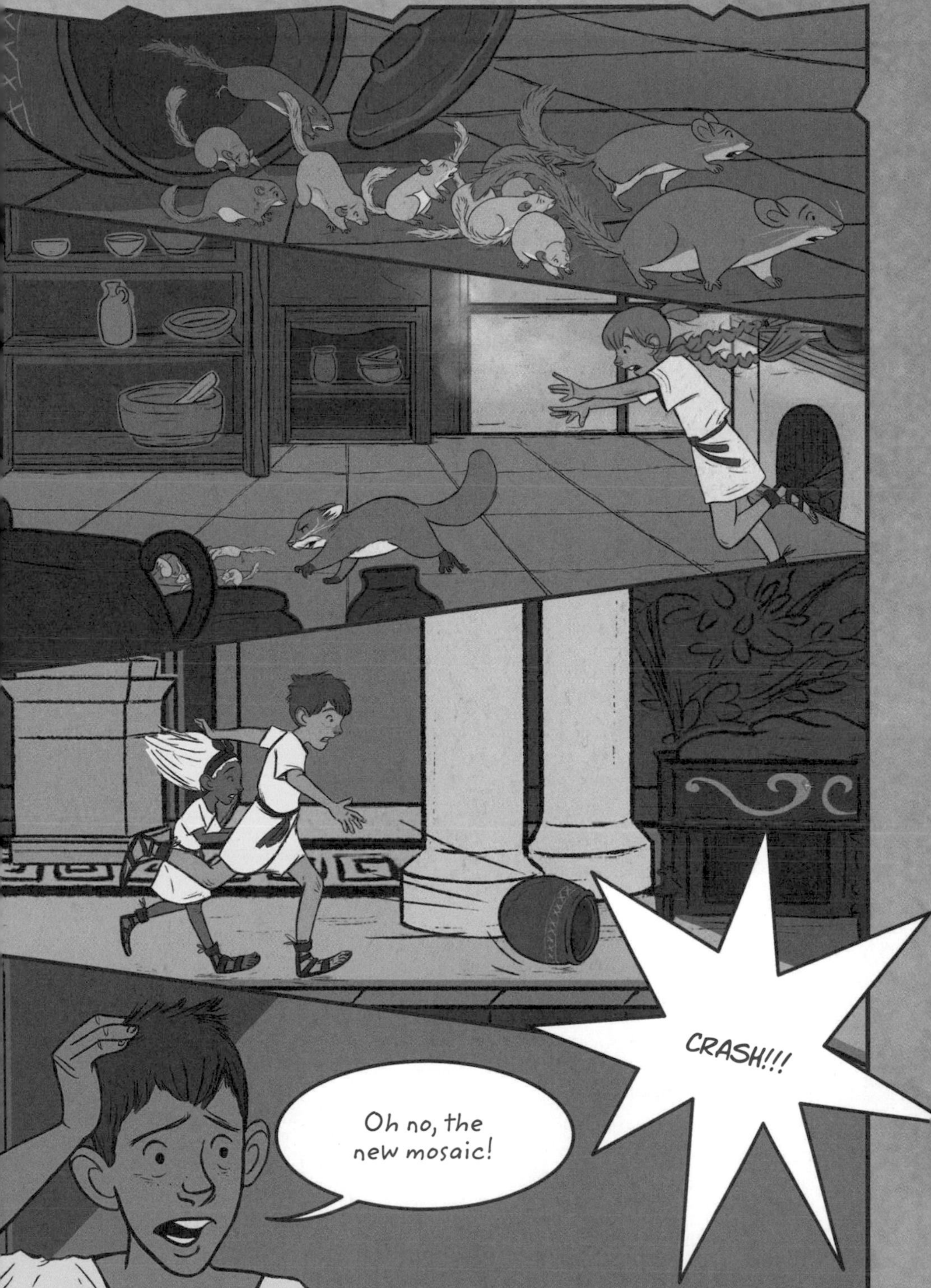
CRASH!!!
Oh no, the new mosaic!

Mosaics

- Mosaics are a form of decoration inside Roman buildings.

- They are pictures made of tiny tiles called **tesserae**.

- Mortar holds the tesserae in place once it has dried.

- Very skilled craftspeople make mosaics of all kinds.

- Rich Romans are very proud of the mosaics they have inside their houses.

Help the Histronauts design a mosaic to replace the broken one.

You will need:

- Scissors

- A piece of cardstock large enough for your mosaic

- A pencil

- Colored cardstock cut into small squares (these are your tesserae)

- Glue (this is your mortar)

1. Draw your design onto the cardstock. It can be whatever you like! A rabbit or a dog or a fun pattern or even a loaf of bread.

2. Once you have drawn the design, start to stick the paper tiles onto your mosaic.

3. After the glue has dried, use your mosaic to decorate your room.

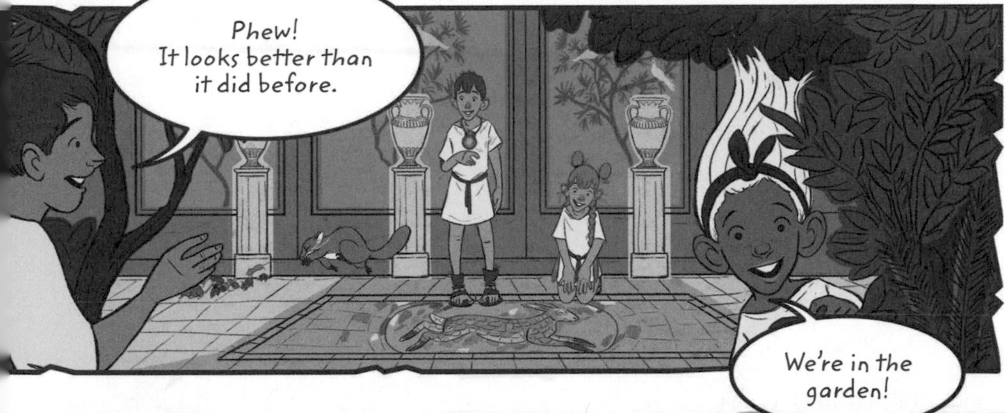
Phew!
It looks better than
it did before.
We're in the
garden!

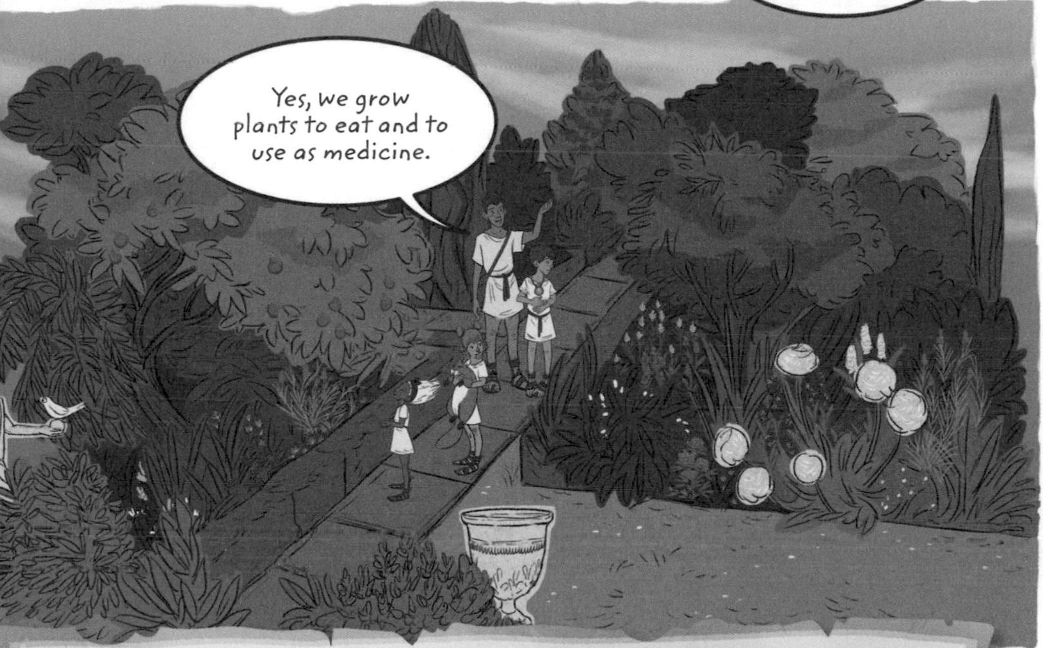
Yes, we grow
plants to eat and to
use as medicine.

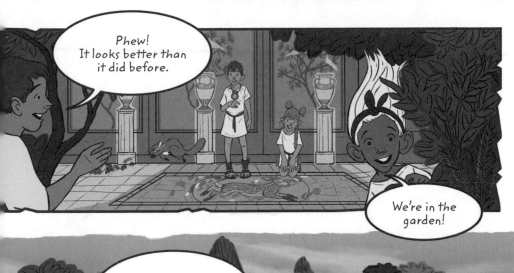

How a Roman garden grows

- The ancient Romans are very proud of their gardens.
- A garden is like an extra room in the house.
- Many of the plants you see in a Roman garden are just like the ones you can find in your garden or nearby park.
- Roses, marigolds, hyacinths, violets, thyme, and rosemary are all common plants in Roman times.
- They also grow fruits and vegetables that are still around today, such as asparagus, leeks, garlic, onions, lettuce, and cucumbers.

Romans used certain plants from their gardens as medicine.

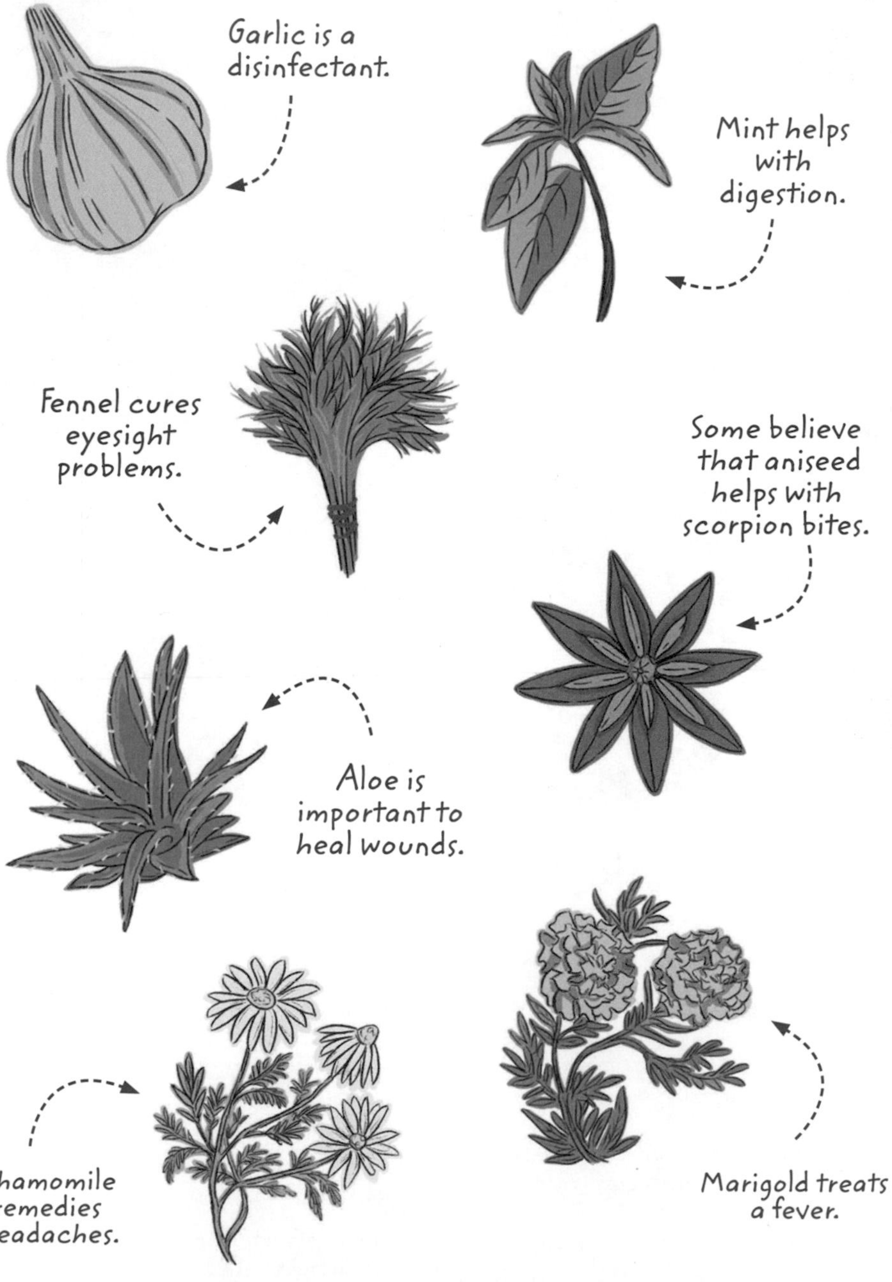
Garlic is a disinfectant.
Mint helps with digestion.
Fennel cures eyesight problems.
Some believe that aniseed helps with scorpion bites.
Aloe is important to heal wounds.
Chamomile remedies headaches.
Marigold treats a fever.

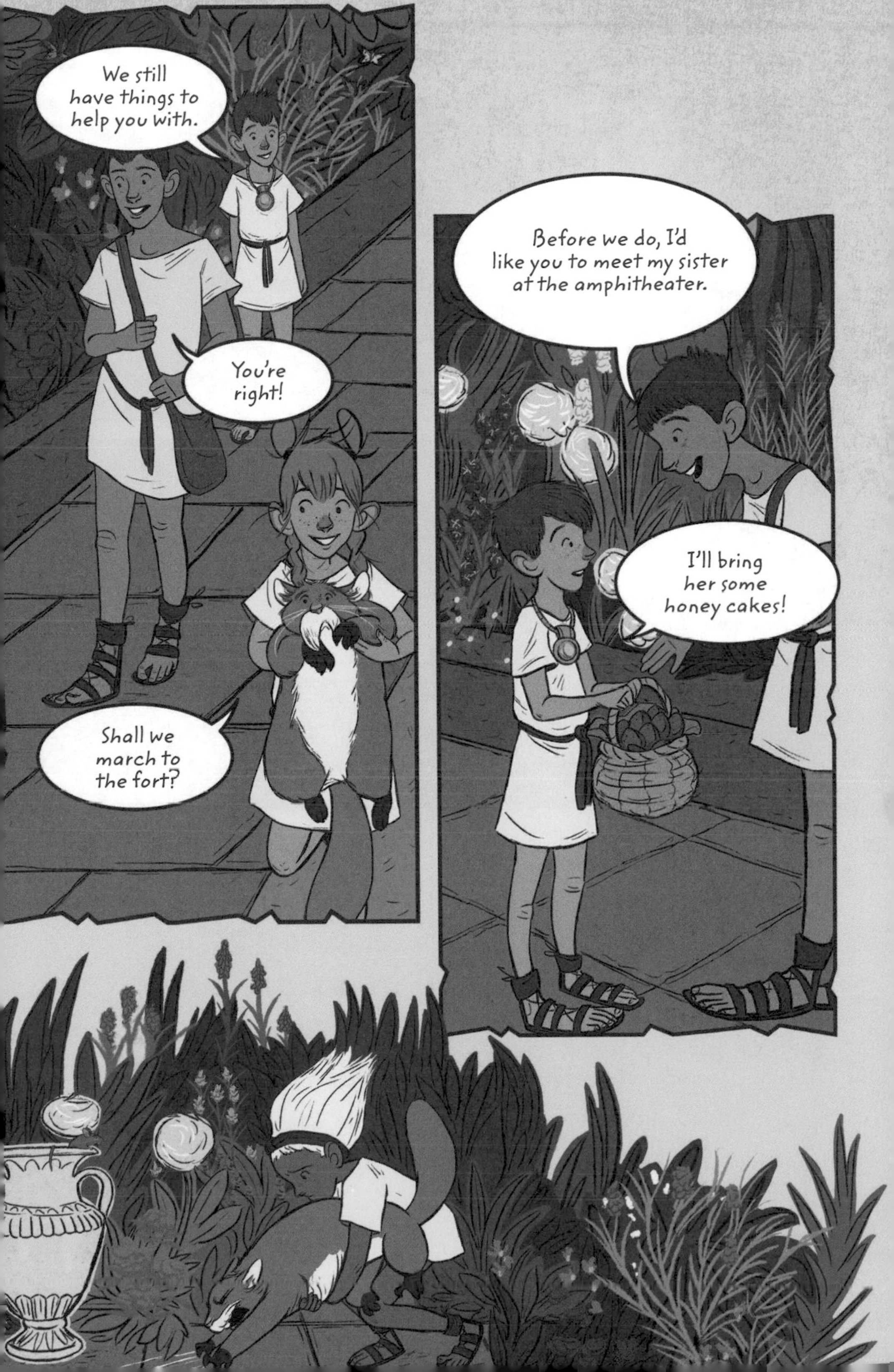

We still have things to help you with.
You're right!
Shall we march to the fort?
Before we do, I'd like you to meet my sister at the amphitheater.
I'll bring her some honey cakes!

An audience inside the amphitheater

My sister works in here.

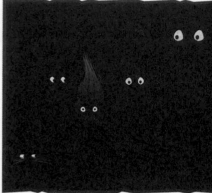

Where are we?

This is the back of the amphitheater.

- Amphitheaters are arena buildings in ancient Rome.

- They are the centers of entertainment.

- Thousands of people come here to watch sports and fighting.

- Some amphitheaters are round and some are oval.

- The biggest ones have room for 50,000 people.

- Romans watch chariot races, gladiator fights, executions, and recreations of great battles.

- Some organizers flood amphitheaters with water so that prisoners can act out sea battles for spectators.

- The Colosseum in Rome is a famous example of an amphitheater.

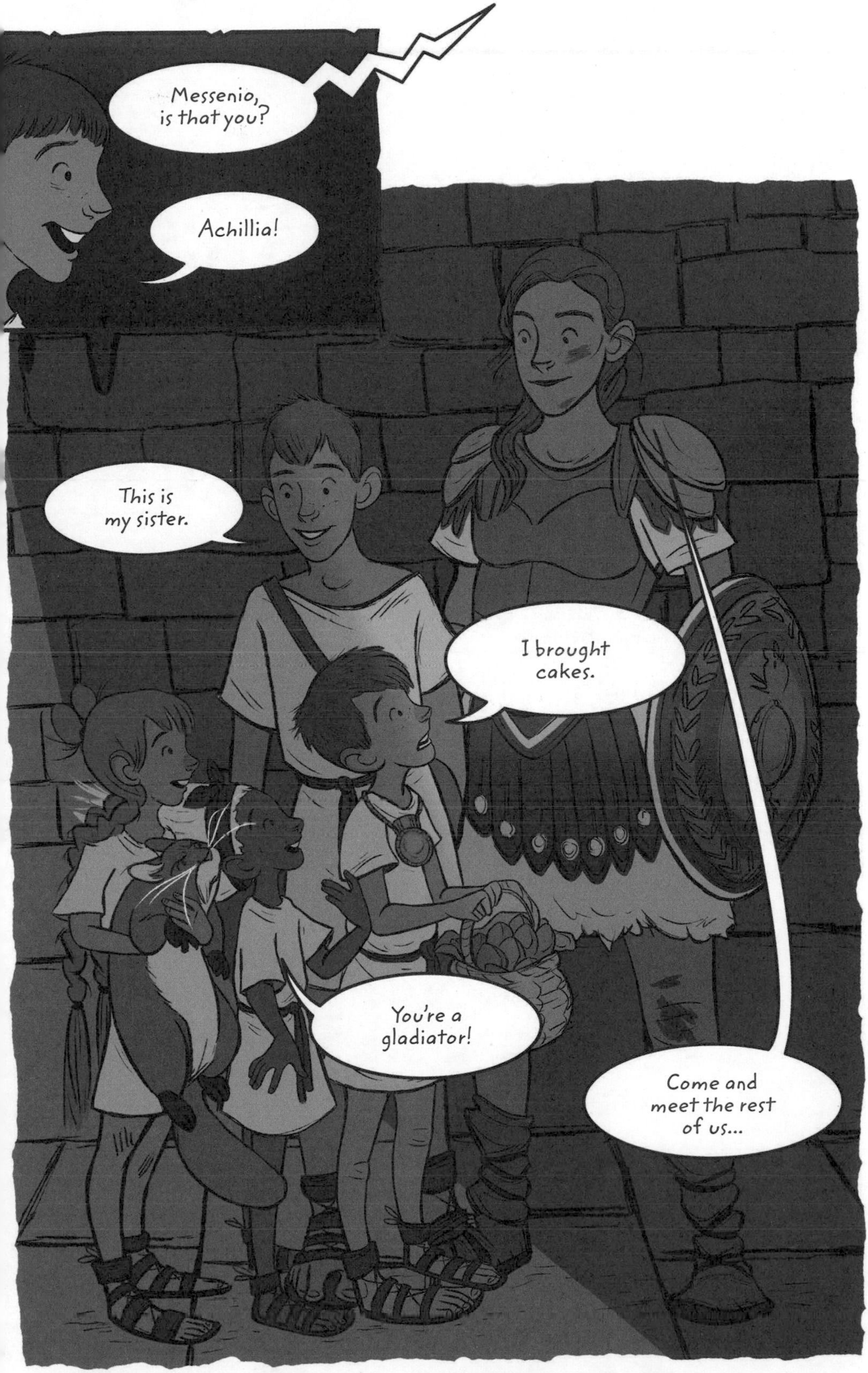
Messenio, is that you?
Achillia!
This is my sister.
I brought cakes.
You're a gladiator!
Come and meet the rest of us...

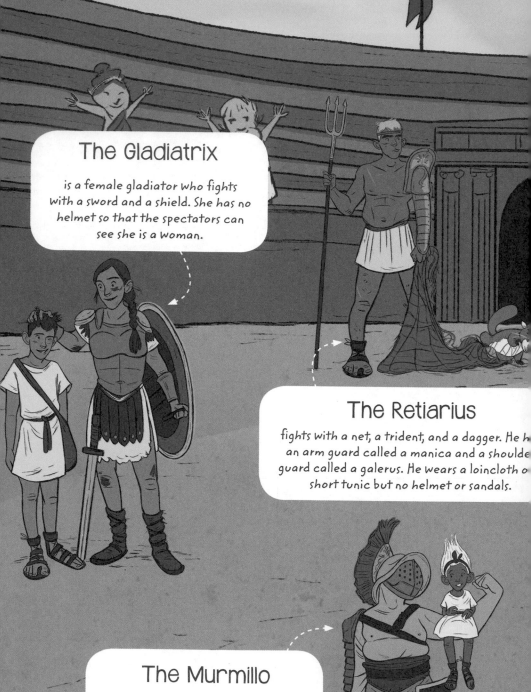

The Gladiatrix

is a female gladiator who fights with a sword and a shield. She has no helmet so that the spectators can see she is a woman.

The Retiarius

fights with a net, a trident, and a dagger. He h an arm guard called a manica and a shoulde guard called a galerus. He wears a loincloth o short tunic but no helmet or sandals.

The Murmillo

fights with a sword and a tall, oblong shield called a scutum. He wears a loincloth, a belt, and a gaiter on his right leg. His helmet has a grill-like face visor.

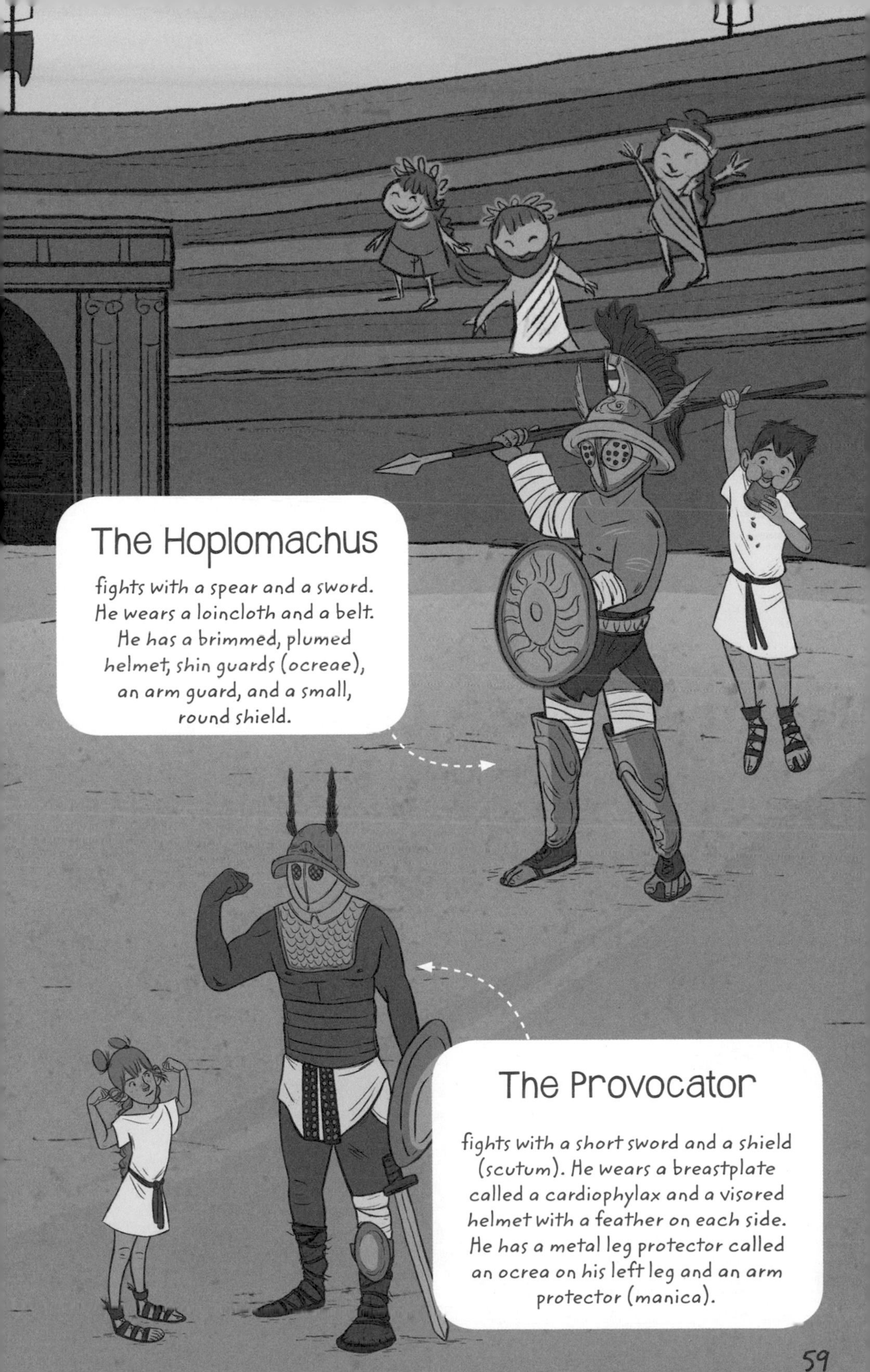

The Hoplomachus

fights with a spear and a sword. He wears a loincloth and a belt. He has a brimmed, plumed helmet, shin guards (ocreae), an arm guard, and a small, round shield.

The Provocator

fights with a short sword and a shield (scutum). He wears a breastplate called a cardiophylax and a visored helmet with a feather on each side. He has a metal leg protector called an ocrea on his left leg and an arm protector (manica).

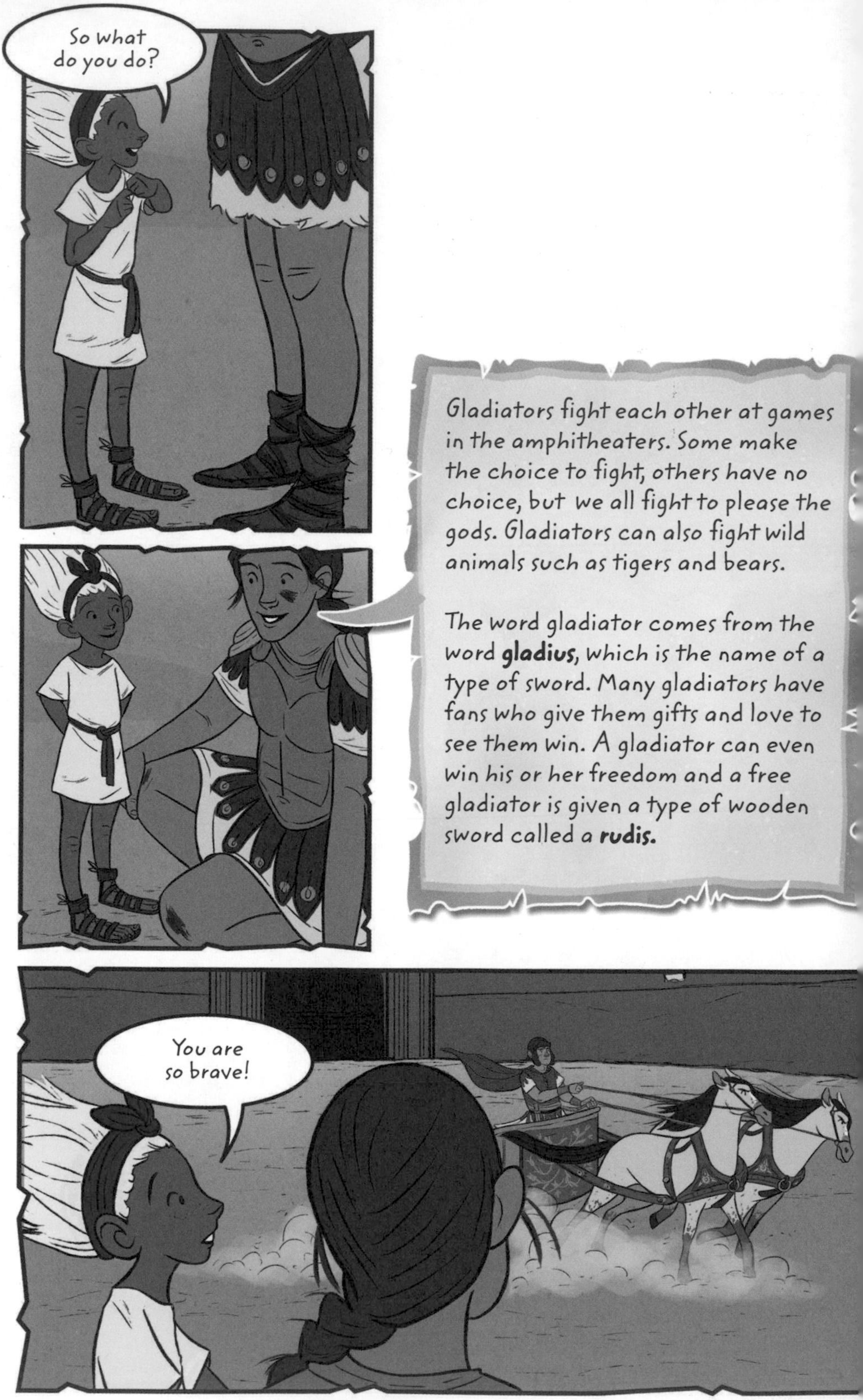
So what do you do?
Gladiators fight each other at games in the amphitheaters. Some make the choice to fight, others have no choice, but we all fight to please the gods. Gladiators can also fight wild animals such as tigers and bears.
The word gladiator comes from the word gladius, which is the name of a type of sword. Many gladiators have fans who give them gifts and love to see them win. A gladiator can even win his or her freedom and a free gladiator is given a type of wooden sword called a rudis.
You are so brave!

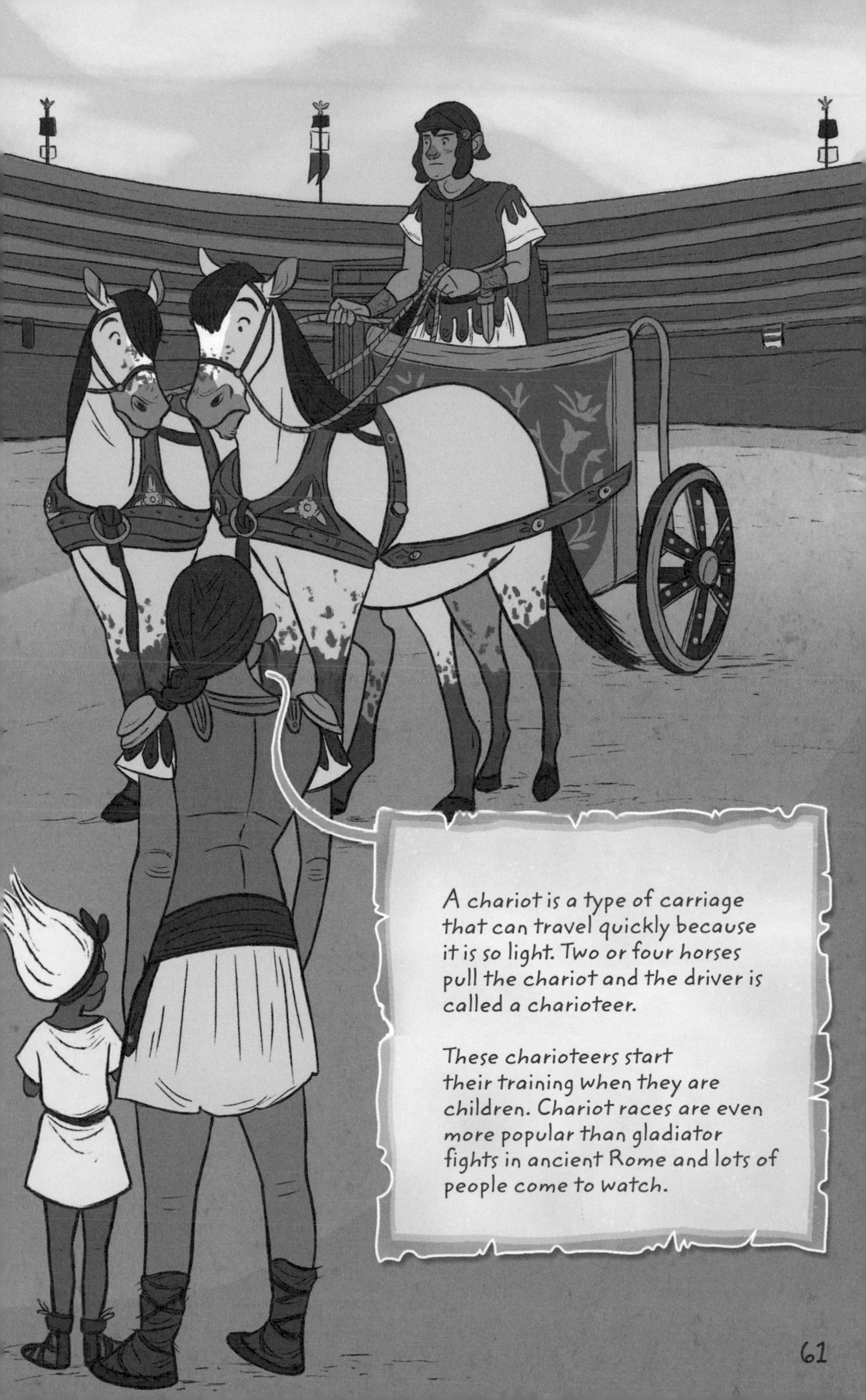
A chariot is a type of carriage that can travel quickly because it is so light. Two or four horses pull the chariot and the driver is called a charioteer.
These charioteers start their training when they are children. Chariot races are even more popular than gladiator fights in ancient Rome and lots of people come to watch.

Build your own chariot

You will need:

- Cardstock
- Glue
- Sticks or string
- Scissors
- Colored pencils

1. Trace the images onto a piece of cardstock and cut out the pieces.

2. Color them in.

3. Fold over the tabs on the main body of the chariot and glue them in place.

4. Stick the wheels into position on either side.

5. Cut out the double horse image, fold at the head, and glue the neck on the inside so it stands up. Make two.

6. Use the string or sticks to fix the horse in front of the chariot.

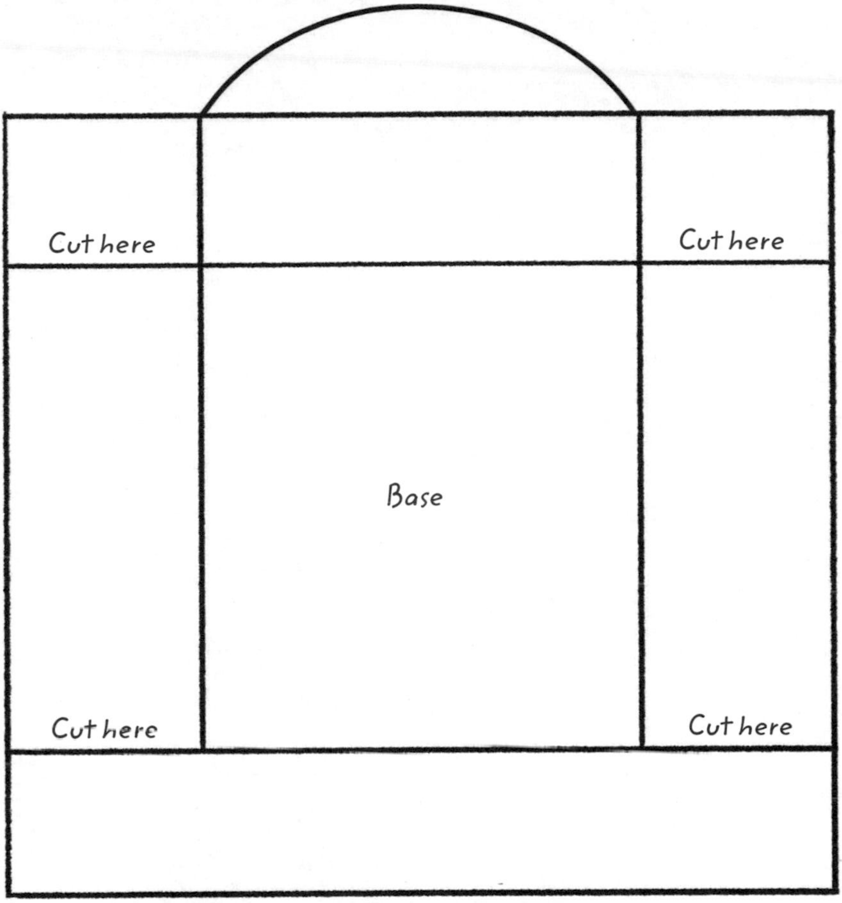
Cut here
Cut here
Base
Cut here
Cut here

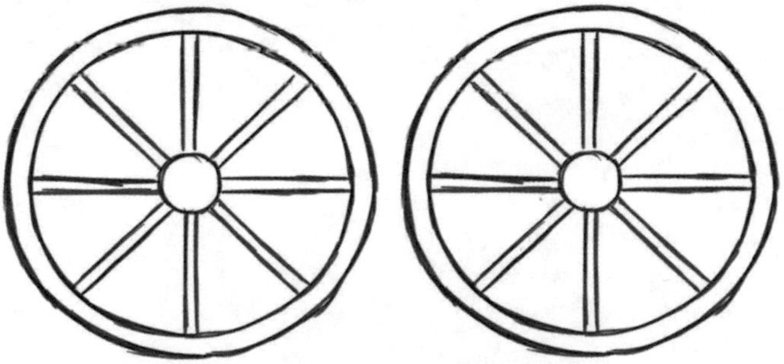

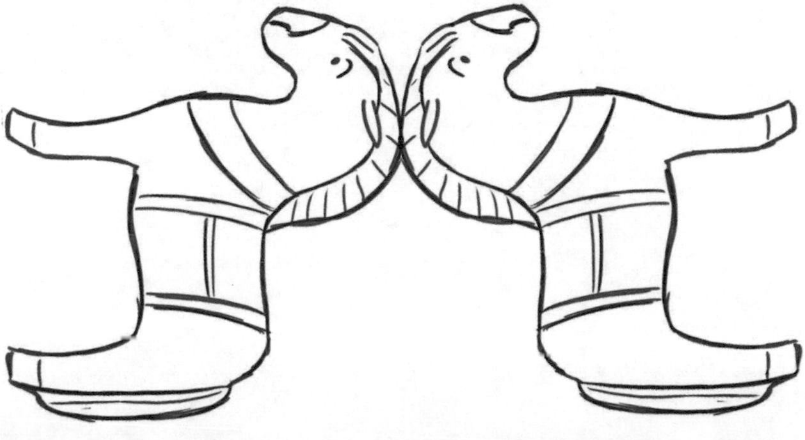

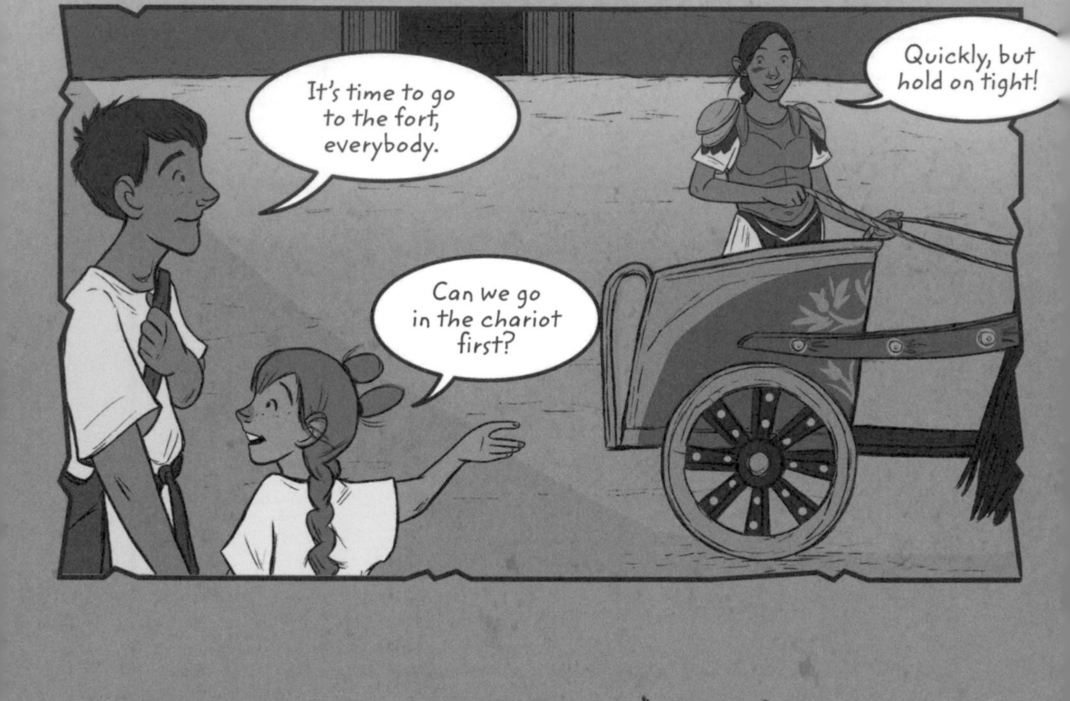
It's time to go to the fort, everybody.
Quickly, but hold on tight!
Can we go in the chariot first?

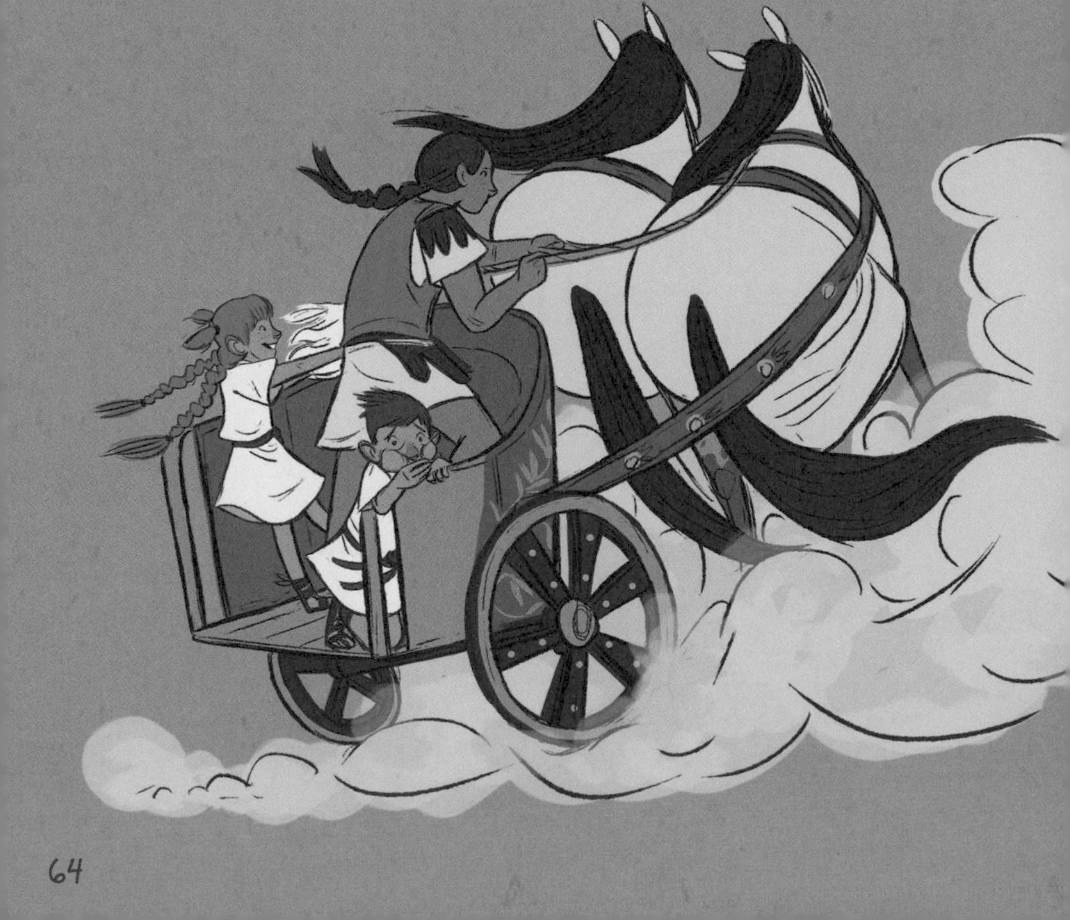

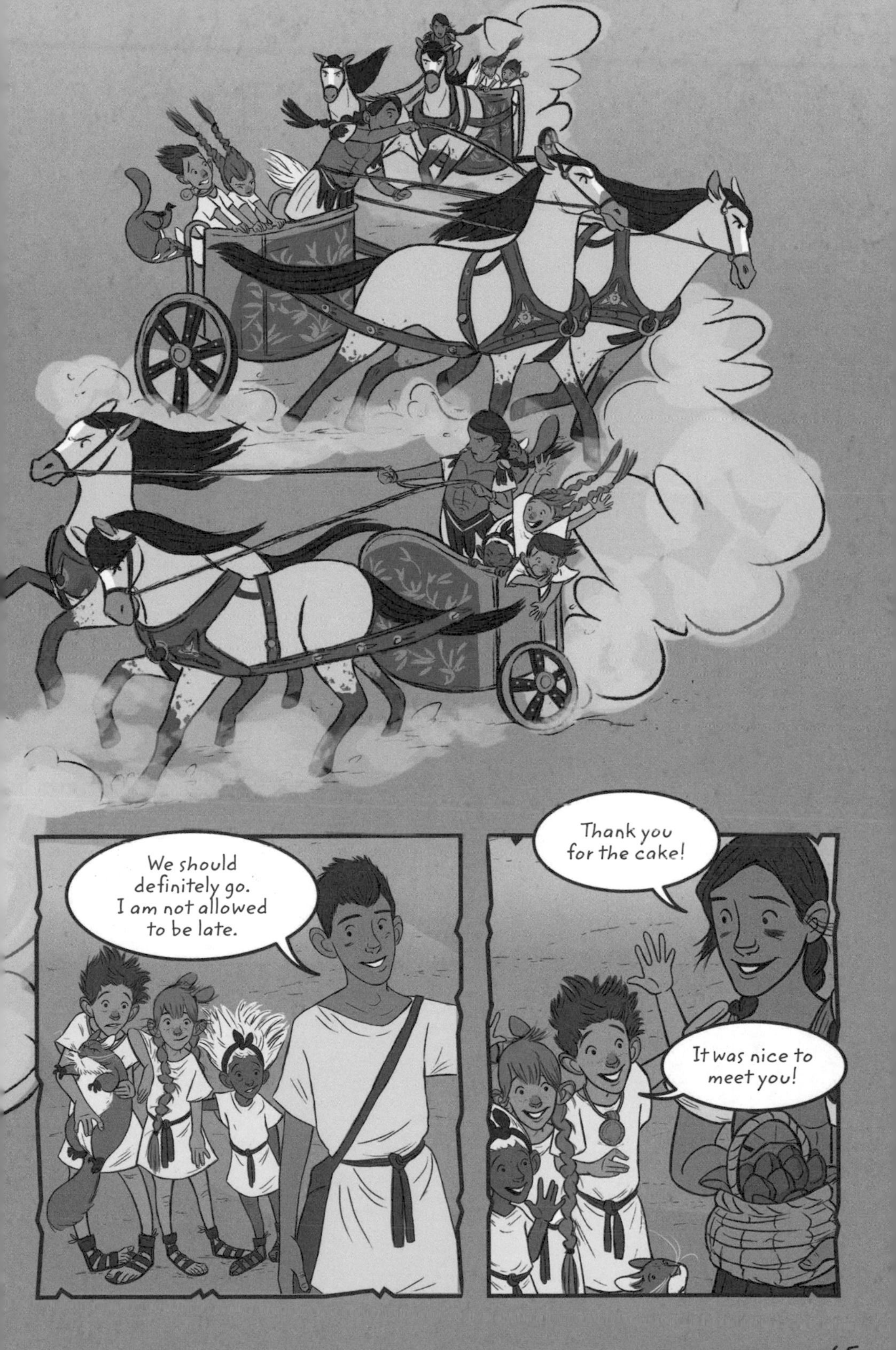
We should definitely go. I am not allowed to be late.
Thank you for the cake!
It was nice to meet you!

The Histronauts invade a Roman fort

- A Roman soldier is called a legionary.
- A centurion is the soldier in charge of a group of legionaries.
- Roman soldiers are always men who are usually also Roman citizens.
- Soldiers have to be over the age of 17 but under the age of 46.
- Most are not allowed to get married.
- They join the army for 25 years.
- After their service ends, they receive a pension.
- Non-Roman citizens can join the army as auxiliary soldiers.

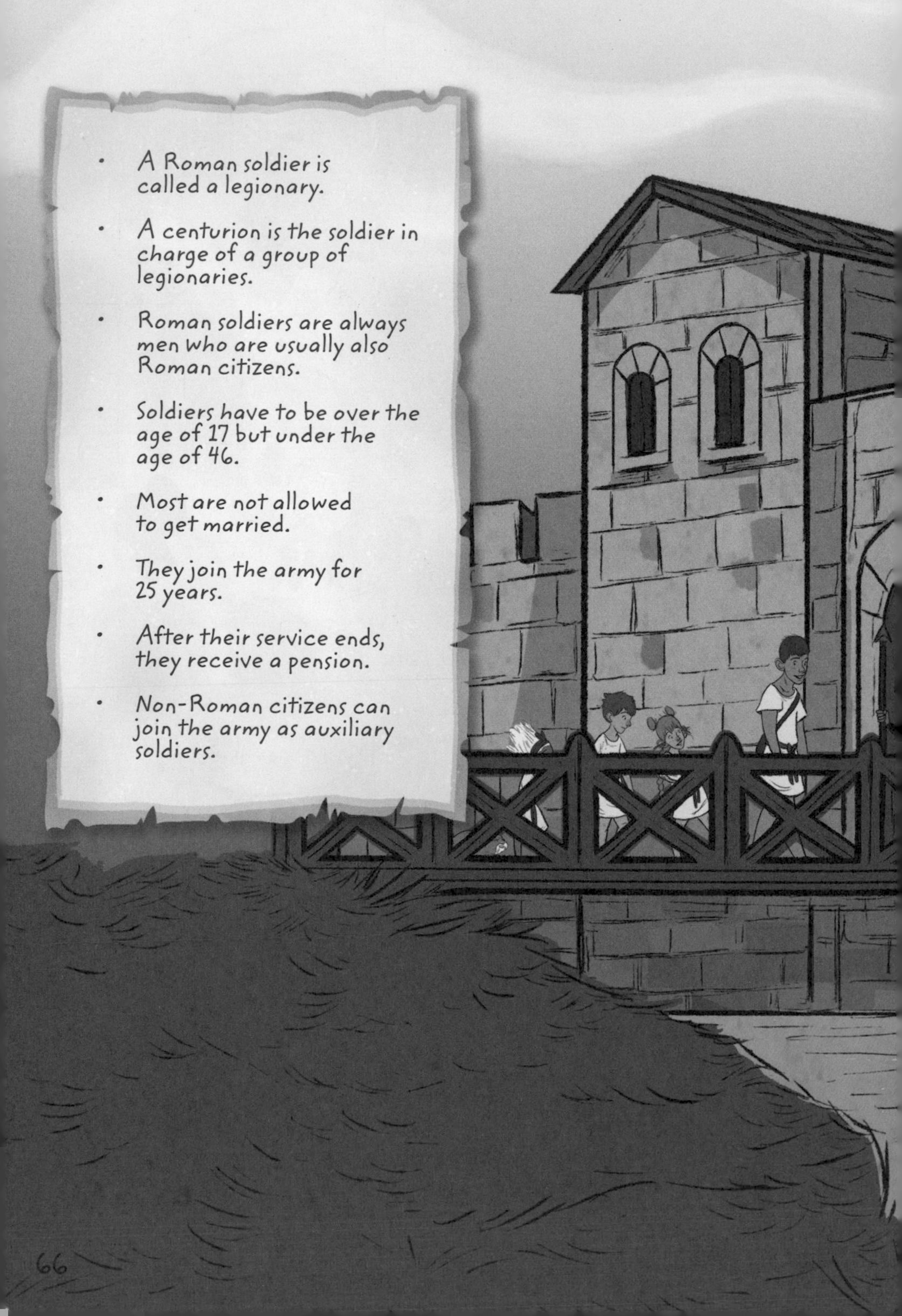

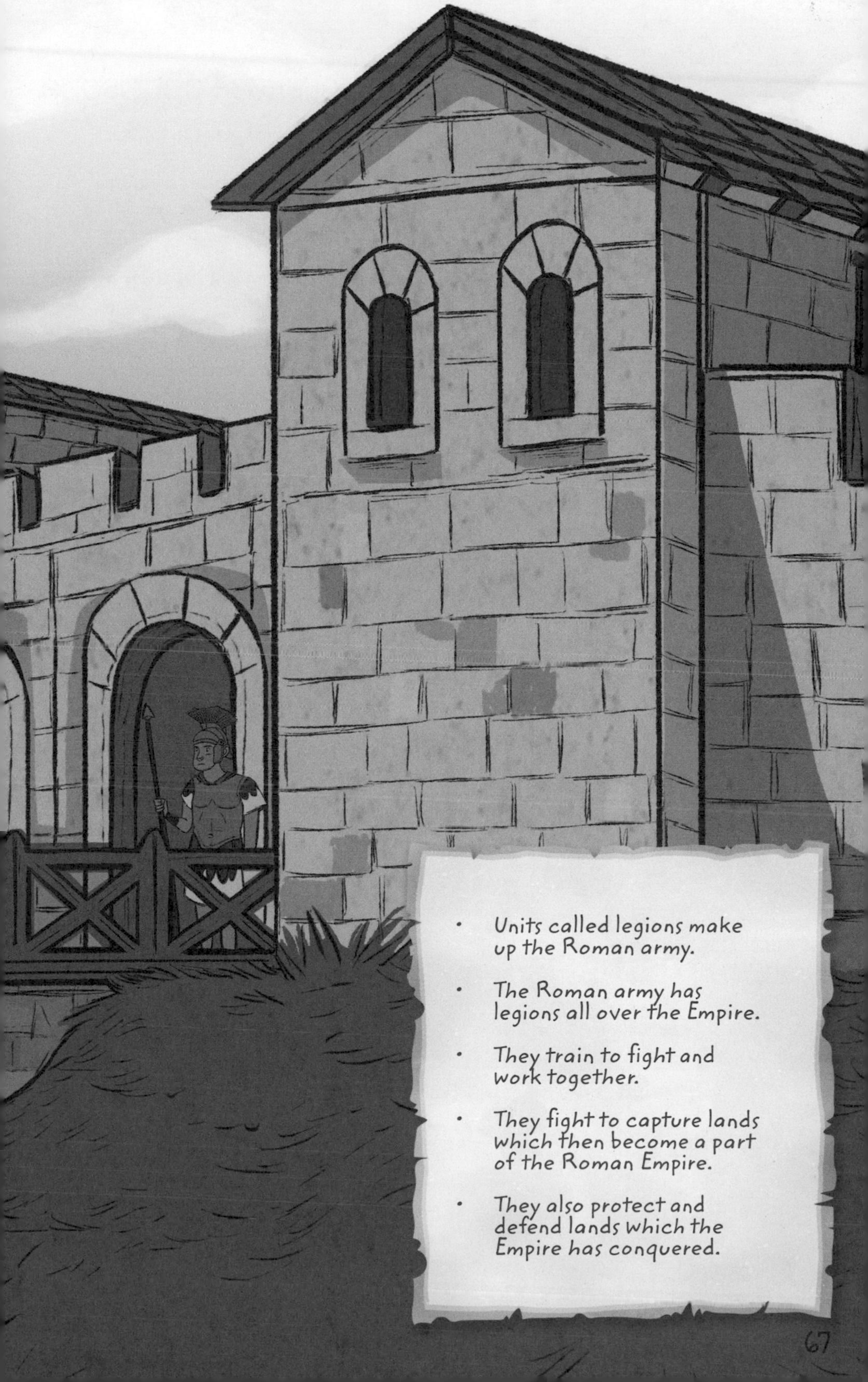

- Units called legions make up the Roman army.
- The Roman army has legions all over the Empire.
- They train to fight and work together.
- They fight to capture lands which then become a part of the Roman Empire.
- They also protect and defend lands which the Empire has conquered.

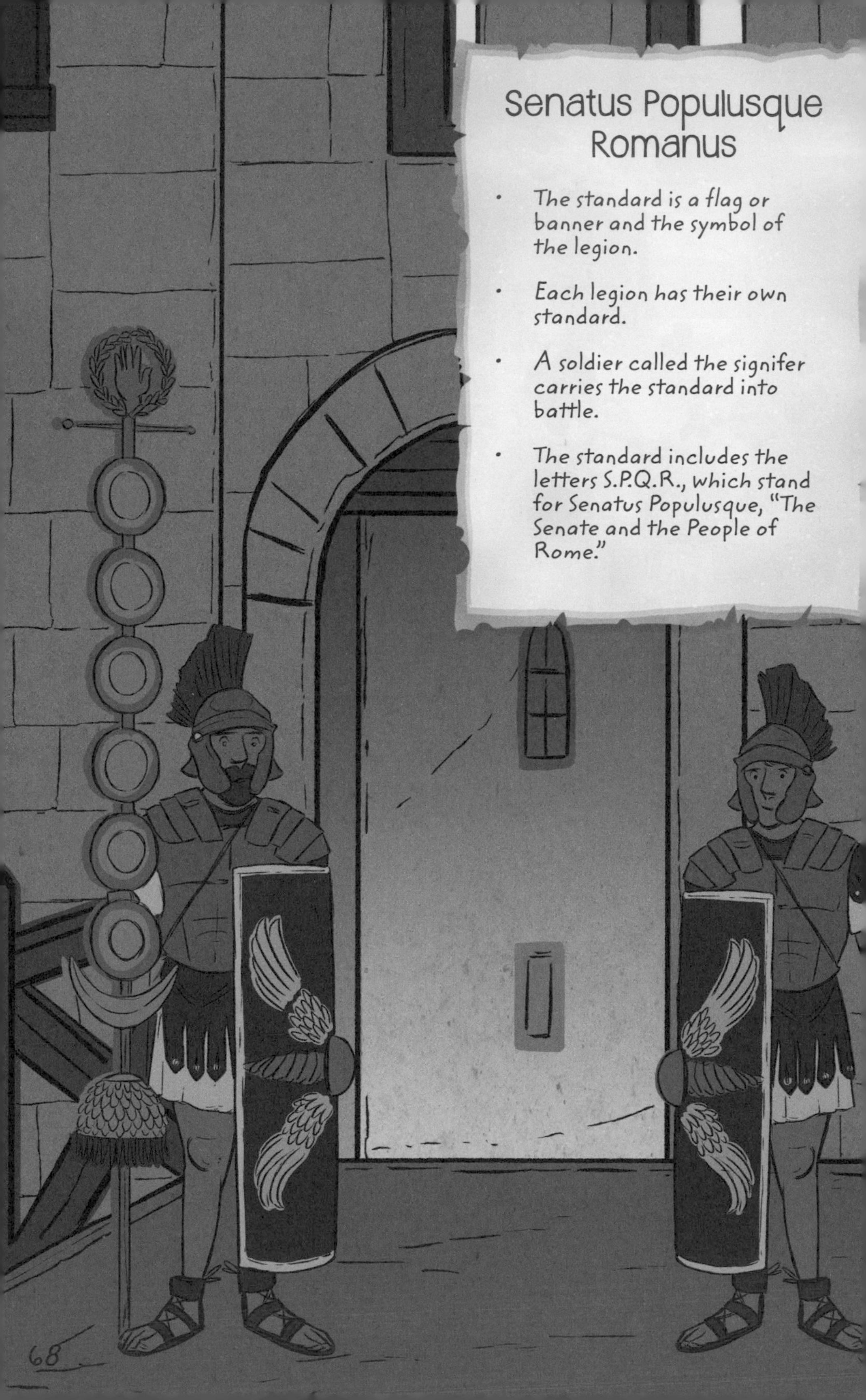

Senatus Populusque Romanus

- The standard is a flag or banner and the symbol of the legion.
- Each legion has their own standard.
- A soldier called the signifer carries the standard into battle.
- The standard includes the letters S.P.Q.R., which stand for Senatus Populusque, "The Senate and the People of Rome."

Design your own Roman standard

Different legions have their own standards with different symbols.

Some standards have a **vexillum** (flag) that shows the unit's number.

A popular symbol for a legion is the **aquila**, or eagle.

The **manus** is a hand that symbolizes the soldiers' oath to the army.

The **draco** is a dragon made of fabric which sails in the wind.

Other standards have an **imago**, which is an image of the emperor.

Design and color your own standard to represent a legion you might belong to. What symbols would you use?

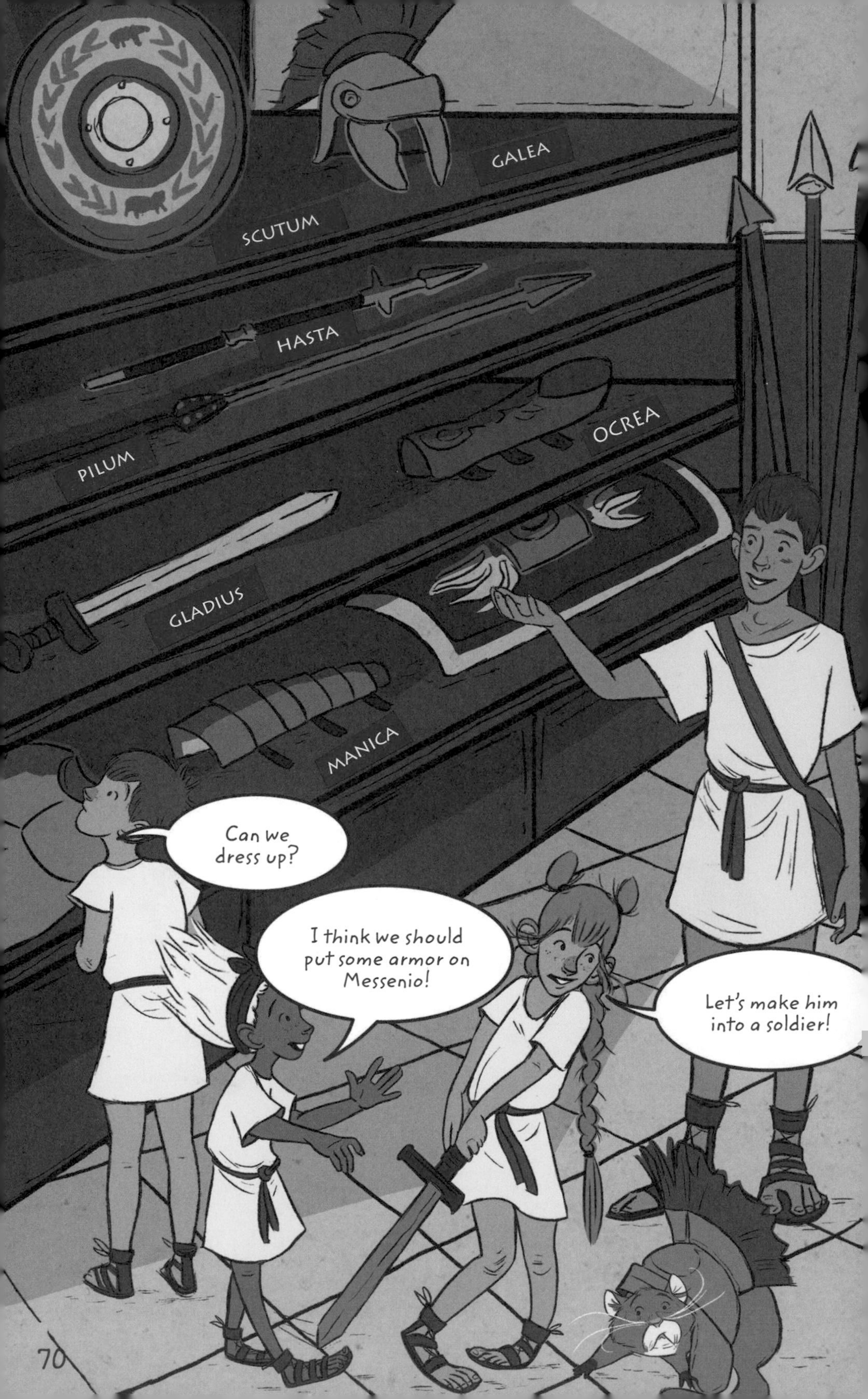
GALEA
SCUTUM
HASTA
PILUM
OCREA
GLADIUS
MANICA
Can we dress up?
I think we should put some armor on Messenio!
Let's make him into a soldier!

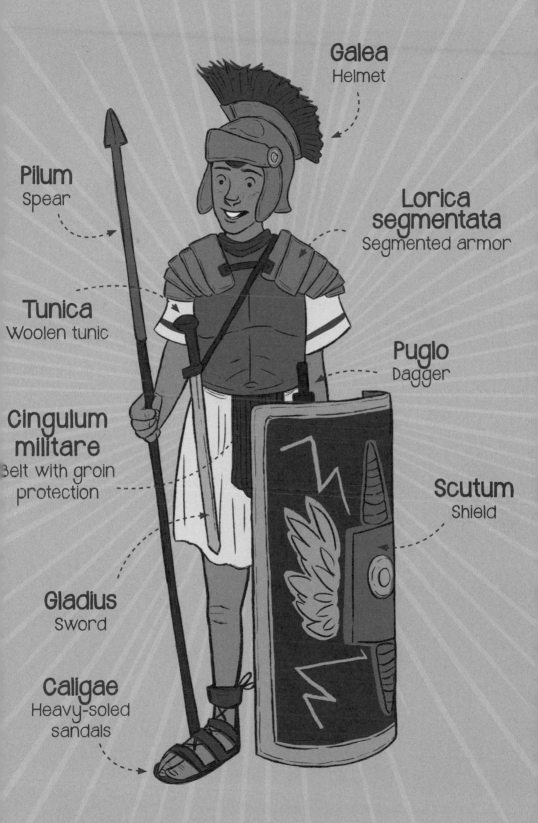

Galea
Helmet

Pilum
Spear

Lorica
segmentata
Segmented armor

Tunica
Woolen tunic

Pugio
Dagger

Cingulum
militare
Belt with groin
protection

Scutum
Shield

Gladius
Sword

Caligae
Heavy-soled
sandals

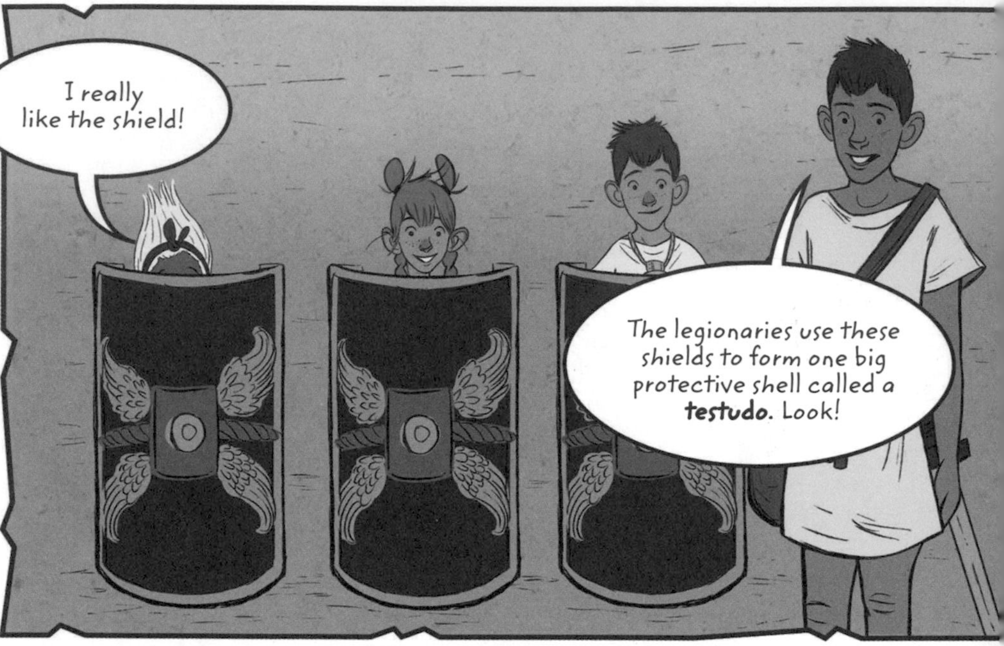
I really like the shield!
The legionaries use these shields to form one big protective shell called a **testudo**. Look!

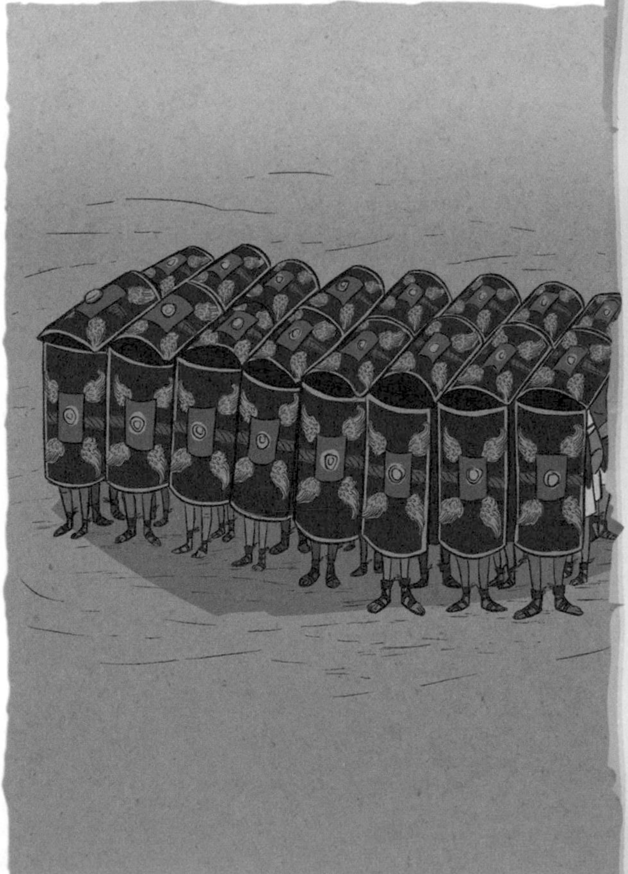

Special maneuvers

- Testudo is the Latin word for tortoise.
- Roman soldiers practice working as a team every day.
- This means that they are very effective at fighting their enemies.
- Roman soldiers also learn special skills.
- Some are archers.
- Others use a giant catapult called an **onager**.
- The cavalry are called **equites.**
- With these skills, the Roman army conquered most of Europe.

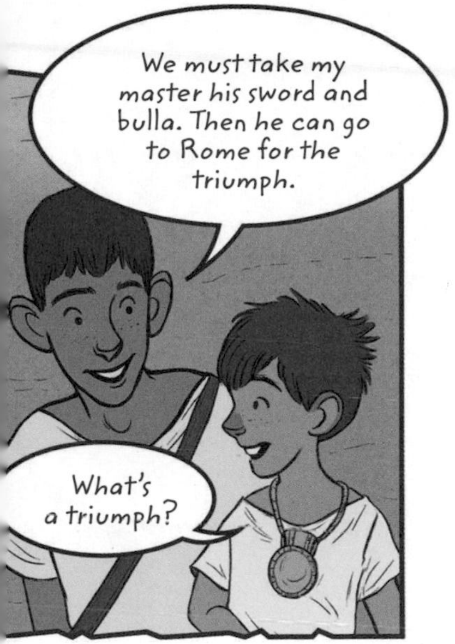
We must take my master his sword and bulla. Then he can go to Rome for the triumph.
What's a triumph?

Victory march

- The triumph is a ceremony that celebrates the success of a general.
- The triumph procession travels through the city to the Temple of Jupiter in Rome.
- The general rides in a chariot pulled by four horses.
- He wears a toga painted gold and purple, a crown of laurel leaves and he wears his bulla to protect him from evil and jealousy.
- Religious ceremonies, banquets, and games at the Colosseum come after the procession.

Make a laurel wreath

You will need:

- Green cardstock
- Scissors
- Glue

What to do:

1. Cut a strip of cardstock long enough to go around your head. Glue it in a circle.
2. Copy the leaf template here onto the cardstock and cut out 10 leaves.
3. Glue the leaves onto the headband.

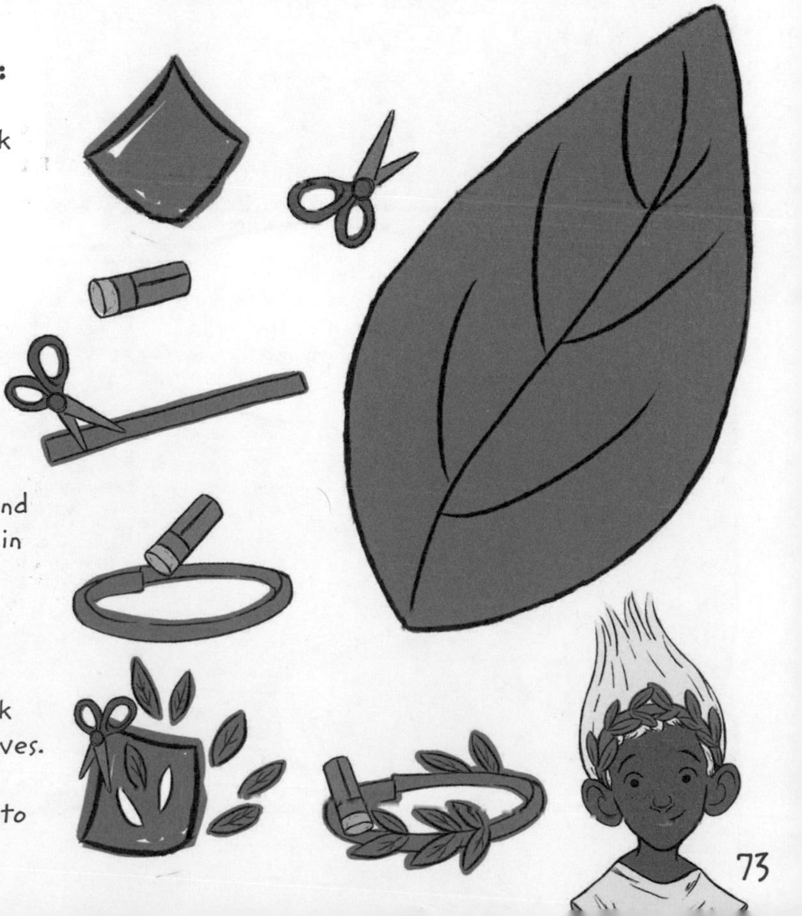

The end of an adventure

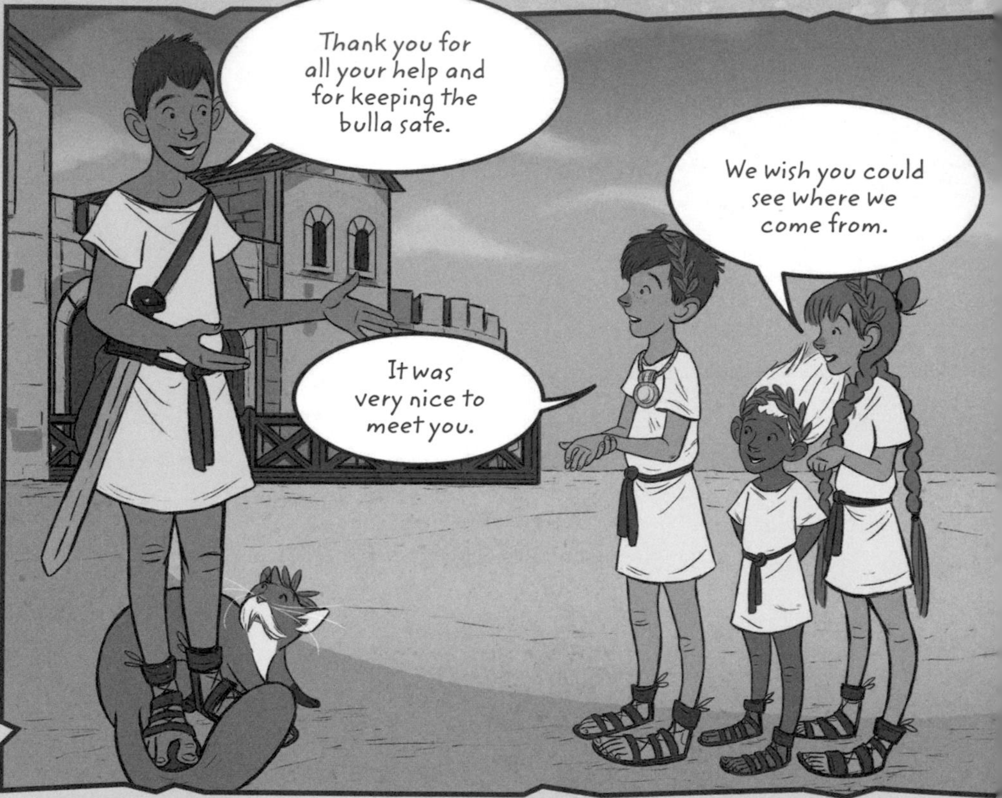
Thank you for all your help and for keeping the bulla safe.
We wish you could see where we come from.
It was very nice to meet you.

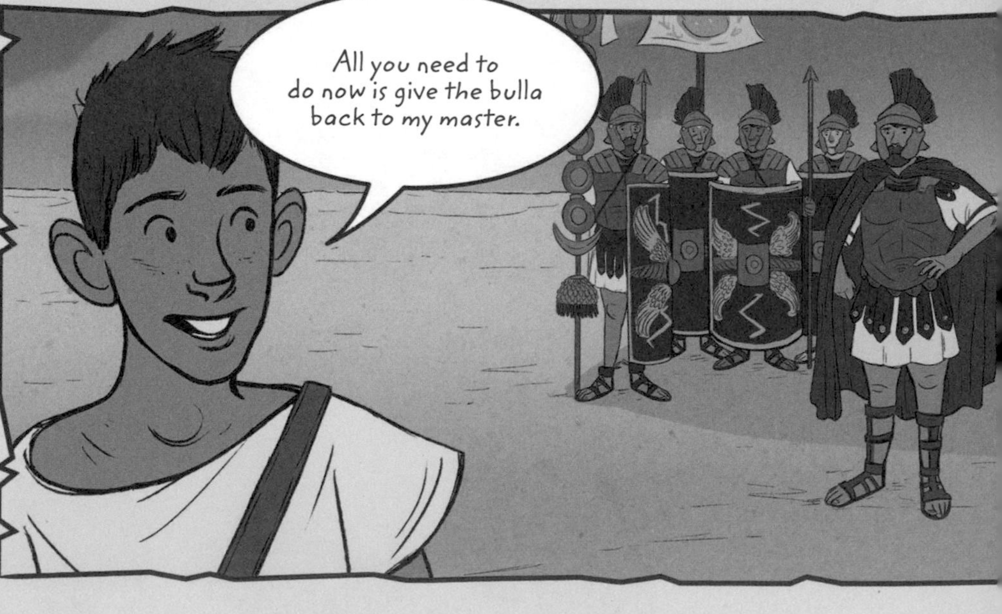
All you need to do now is give the bulla back to my master.

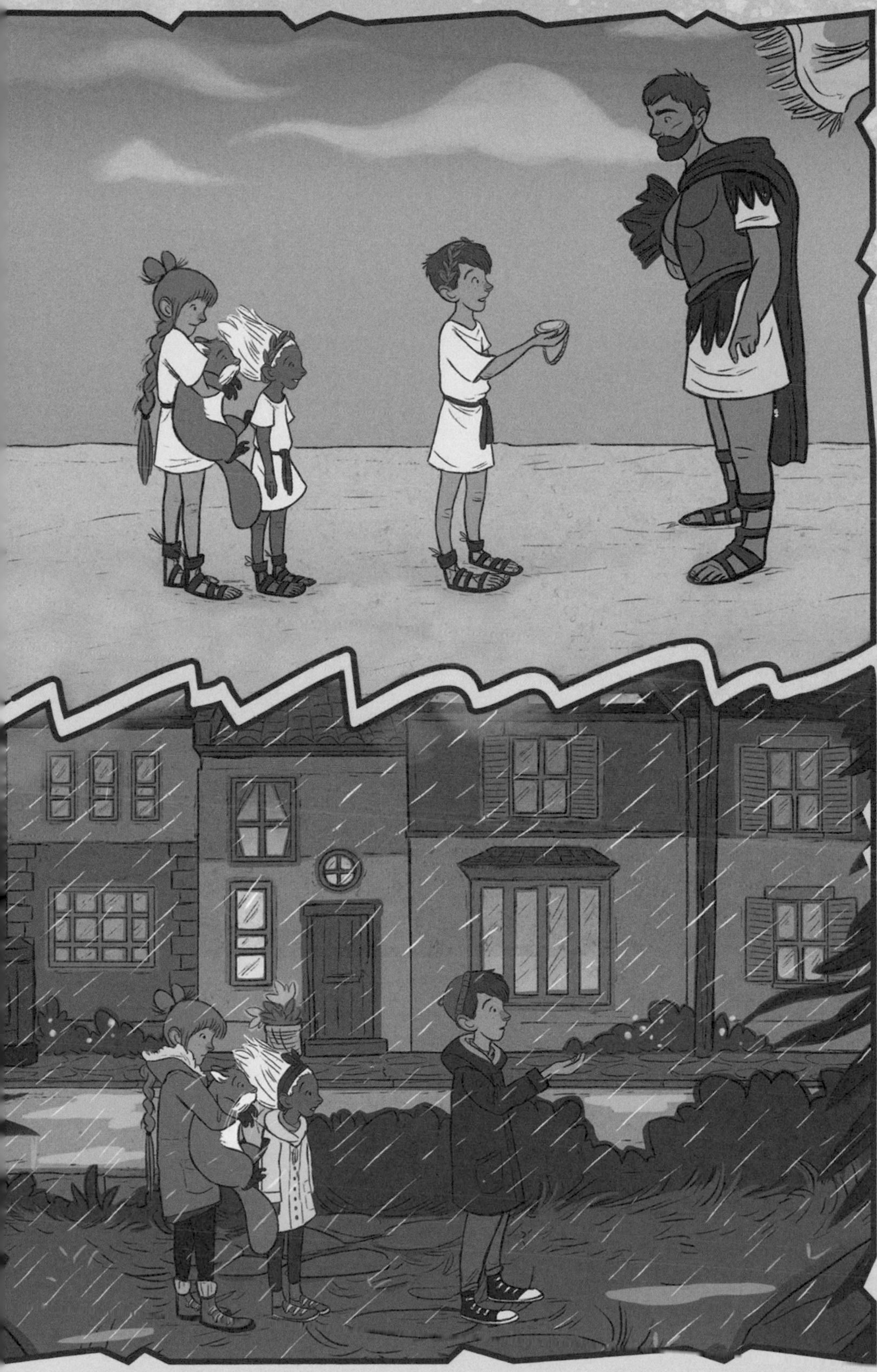

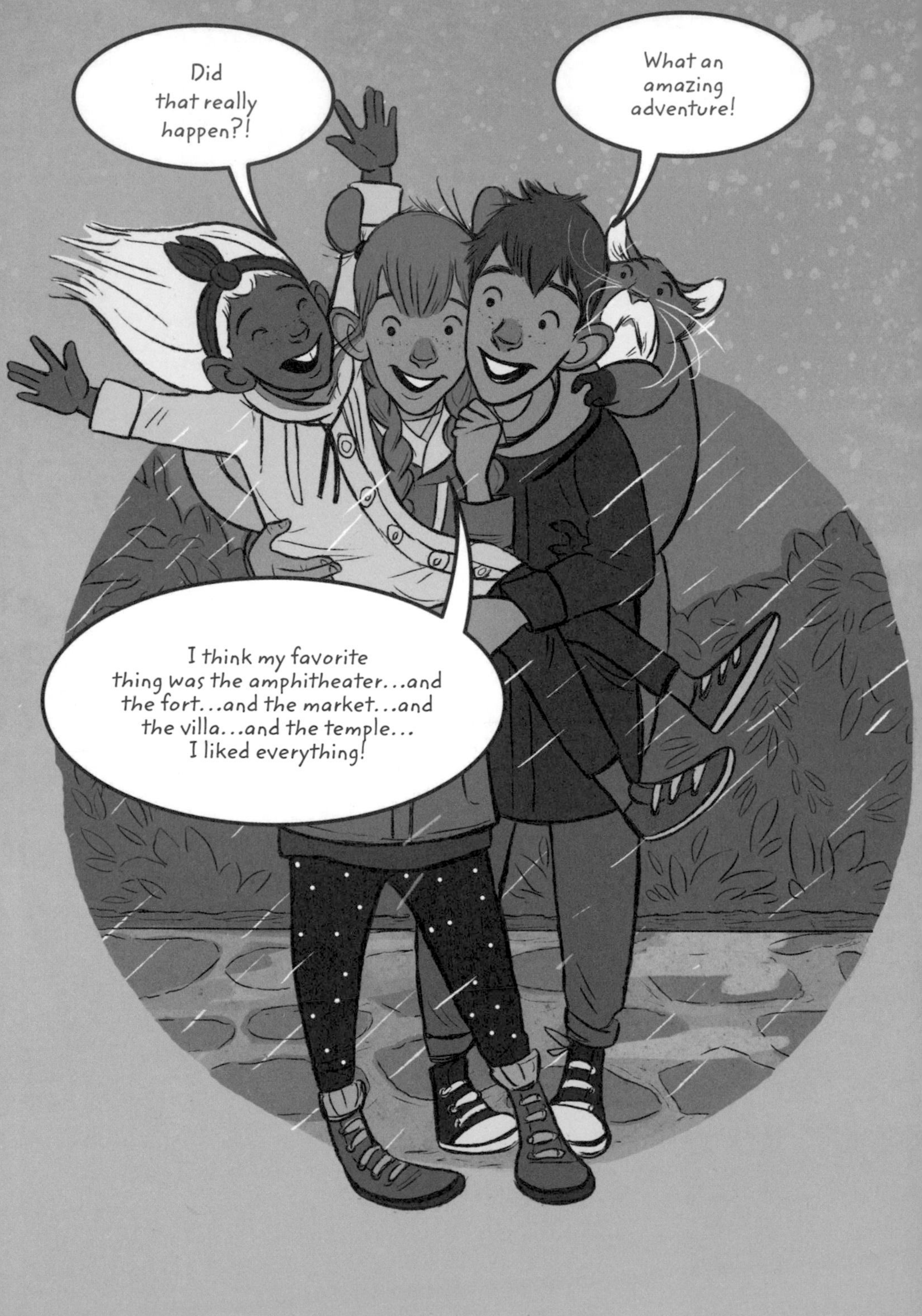
Did that really happen?!
What an amazing adventure!
I think my favorite thing was the amphitheater...and the fort...and the market...and the villa...and the temple... I liked everything!

Quiz questions

1. Which herb heals scorpion bites?

a) peppermint
b) thyme
c) aniseed

2. What type of art uses small tiles?

a) patchwork
b) mosaic
c) collage

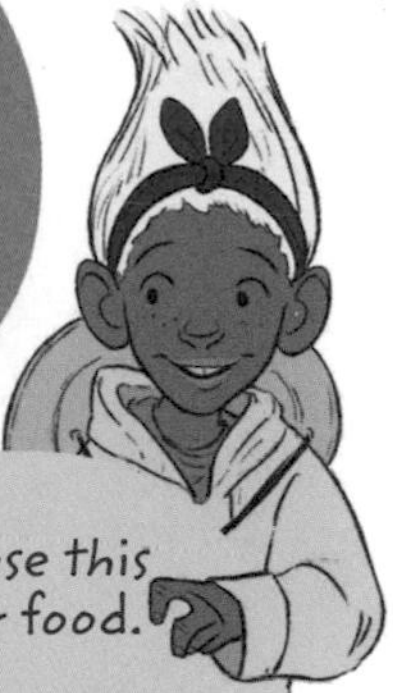

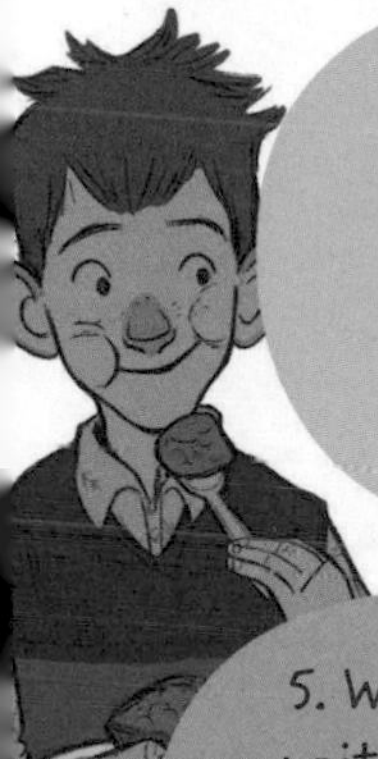

3. What language did the Romans speak?

a) Italian
b) Latin
c) French

4. The Romans use this to sweeten their food.

a) honey
b) lemons
c) figs

5. What is the word for a unit in the Roman army?

a) a legion
b) a battalion
c) a squad

6. What is the name of an outfit that only rich men wear?

a) a poncho
b) a toga
c) a dressing gown

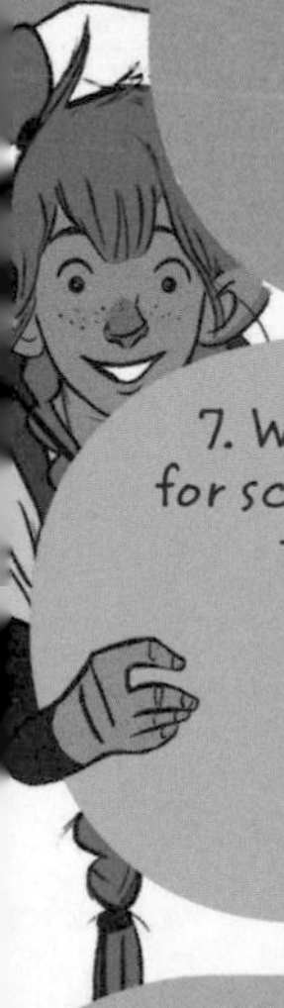

7. Which of these is a tool for scraping oil off the skin in the Roman baths?

a) a scraper
b) a straw
c) a strigil

8. What is the name of the amulet that little boys wear?

a) a bulla
b) a lunula
c) a votive

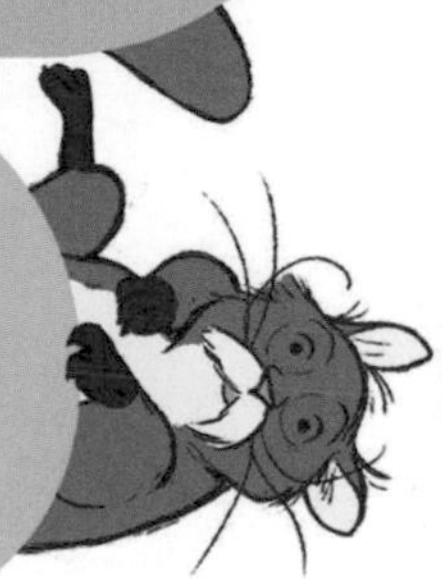

9. What is the name of a Roman gold coin?

a) a euro
b) an aureus
c) a penny

10. What type of shoes did the Romans wear?

a) stilettos
b) espadrilles
c) sandals

Answers

pp. 16–17

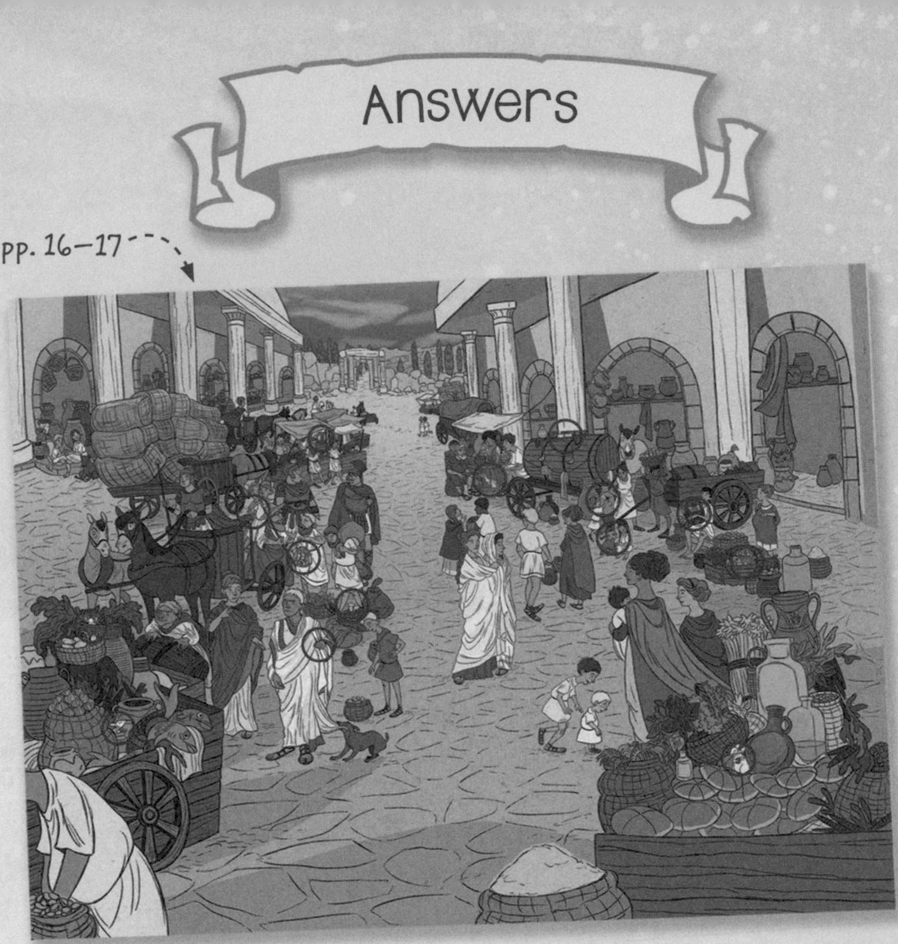

pp. 20-21

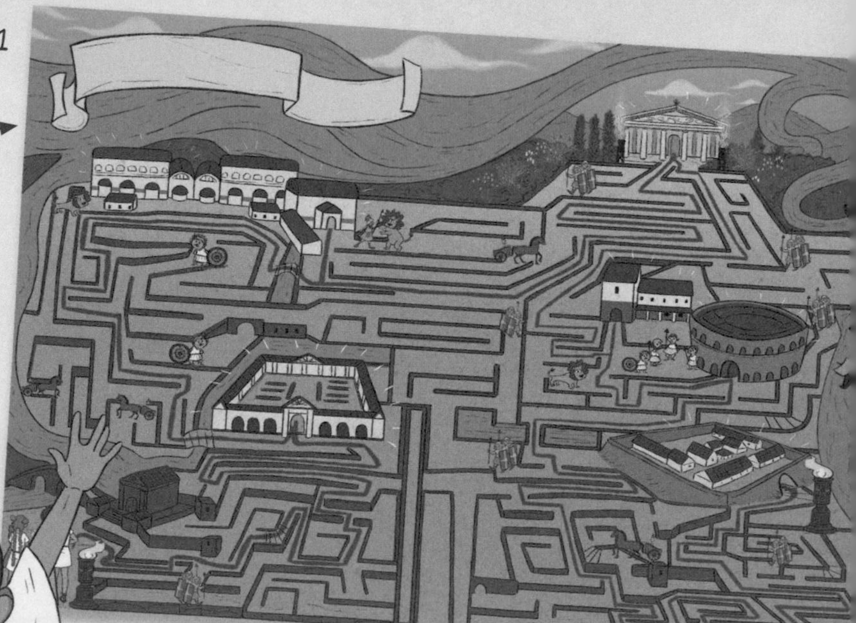

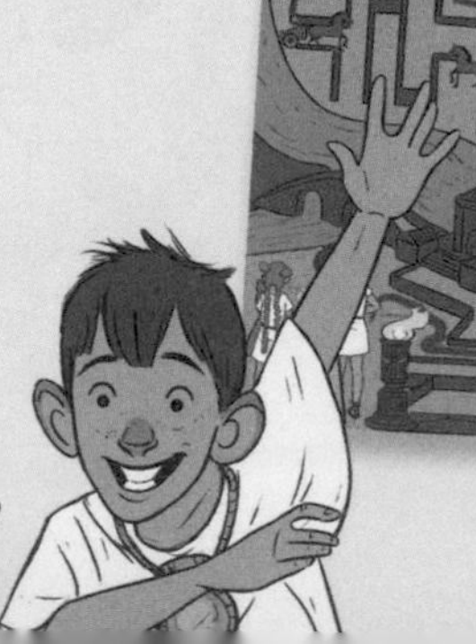

p. 26

LVIII = 58
XXVI = 26
VIII = 8
CCIV = 204

XVIIII = 18
DVI = 506
XLV = 45
MLIII = 1053

22 = XXII
67 = LXVII
5 = V
18 = XVIII

520 = DXX
109 = CIX
99 = XCIX
52 = LII

X + IV = 14
L + III = 53
M + L + X = 1060
D + IV = 504
C + XXVI = 126

X – II = 8
D – LX = 440
V – I = 4
C – XXII = 78
CC – LXXXI = 119

p. 27
Can Messenio buy his shoes?
Yes! There are five denarii left over.

p. 77

1. c) aniseed   2. b) mosaic
3. b) Latin   4. a) honey
5. a) a legion   6. b) a toga
7. c) a strigil 8. a) a bulla
9. b) an aureus 10. c) sandals

How did you do?

GLOSSARY

Amphora
(am-for-a)
Jug

Apodyterium
(apo-dee-tair-ium)
Changing room

Aquila
(ak-wee-la)
Eagle

As
(as)
Copper coin

Atrium
(ay-tree-um)
Entrance to the
Roman baths

Aureus
(or-ree-us)
Gold coin

Bulla
(bull-a)
Boy's amulet

Caldarium
(cal-darium)
Hot room

Cena
(kay-na)
Dinner

Denarius
(denarii plural)
(deh-nah-ree-us)
Silver coin

Draco
(drah-ko)
Dragon

Dulcia
(dul-kia)
Dessert

Equites
(ek-wit-ays)
Cavalry

Forum
(four-um)
Marketplace

Frigidarium
(fri-jid-arium)
Cold room

Galea
(gay-lee-a)
Helmet

Gladius
(glad-ee-us)
Sword

Hasta
(ha-stah)
Spear

Hypocaust
(hi-po-cawst)
Underfloor heating

Ientaculum
(ien-tak-ulum)
Breakfast

Imago
(im-may-go)
Icon of the Emperor

Klinai
(klin-eye)
Sofa

Libertus
(lee-bur-tus)
Free slave

Lunula
(lun-you-la)
Girl's amulet

Manus
(mah-noos)
Hand

Mensa ponderaria
(men-sah pon-deh-
rah-reea)
Weights and
measures table

Merels
(meh-rels)
Type of game

Onager
(on-a-jer)
Catapult

Palaestra
(pa-lay-stra)
Gym

Pilum
(pill-um)
Javelin/spear

Prandium
(pran-dium)
Lunch

Rudis
(roo-diss)
Wooden sword given
to free gladiators

Sestertius
(seh-ster-shus)
Bronze coin

Stylus
(ss-ty-luss)
Pen

Tabula
(tab-yew-la)
Writing tablet

Tepidarium
(teh-pid-arium)
Warm room

Tesserae
(tess-er-eye)
Mosaic tiles

Testudo
(test-yew-doh)
Tortoise

Thermae
(therm-eye)
Roman baths

Triclinium
(try-klin-eeum)
Formal dining room

Triumph
(try-umf)
Military ceremony

Vexillum
(vex-ill-um)
Flag

Villa
(vil-ah)
Large house

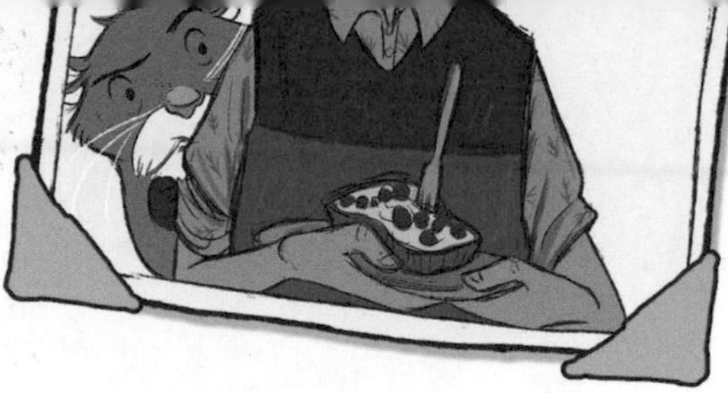

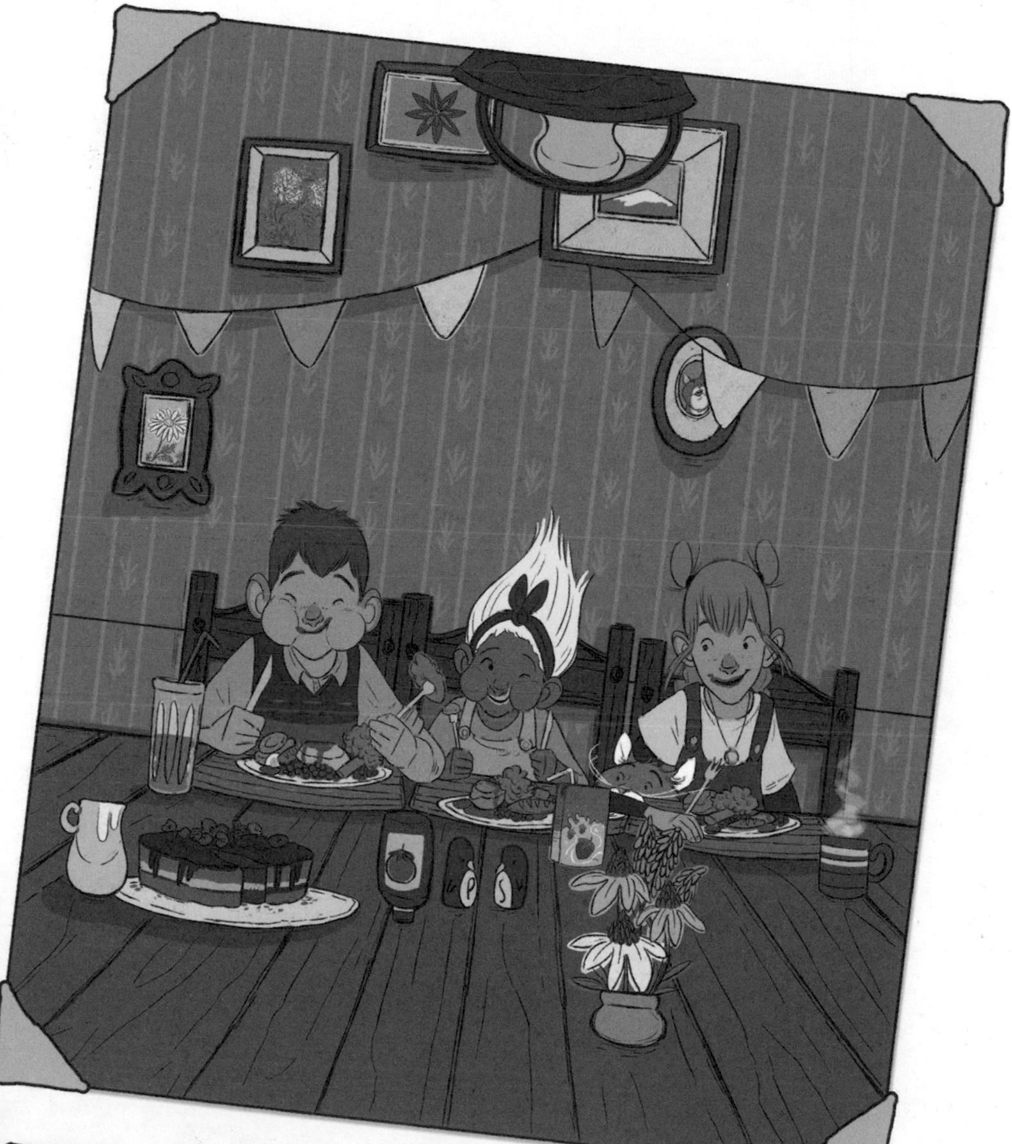

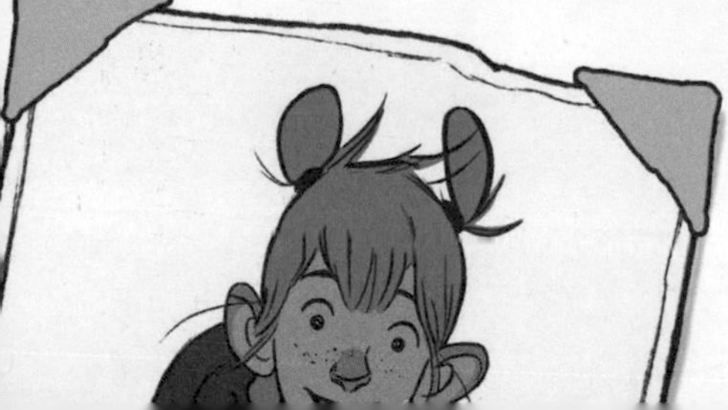

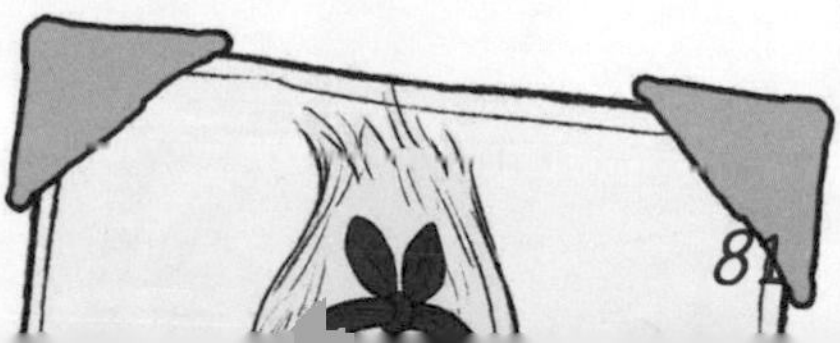

About the author and illustrator

Spot the author and illustrator in the book!

Frances is a historian and dedicated castle visitor. She can usually be found in the library surrounded by stacks of books that she can't wait to read.
Likes: Books, holidays, thunderstorms, trains, and the theater
Dislikes: Washing up
Favorite Color: Purple
Favorite Food: Fish and chips
Favorite Places: Libraries and castles

Grace is an illustrator and animator. She loves to explore with her two dogs, Muffin and Kodie-bear.
Likes: Adventures, the ocean, fairy lights, olives, and animals
Dislikes: Having wet socks
Favorite Color: Turquoise
Favorite Food: Apple crumble
Favorite Places: Forests and outer space

Ready for more adventures with The Histronauts?
Here's a sneak peek of *An Egyptian Adventure*!

THE HISTRONAUTS
AN EGYPTIAN ADVENTURE

Written by
FRANCES DURKIN

Illustrated by
GRACE COOKE

Designed by
VICKY BARKER

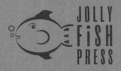

JOLLY FISH PRESS

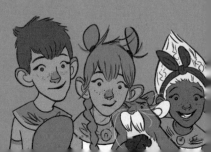

A new friend on the banks of the River Ni

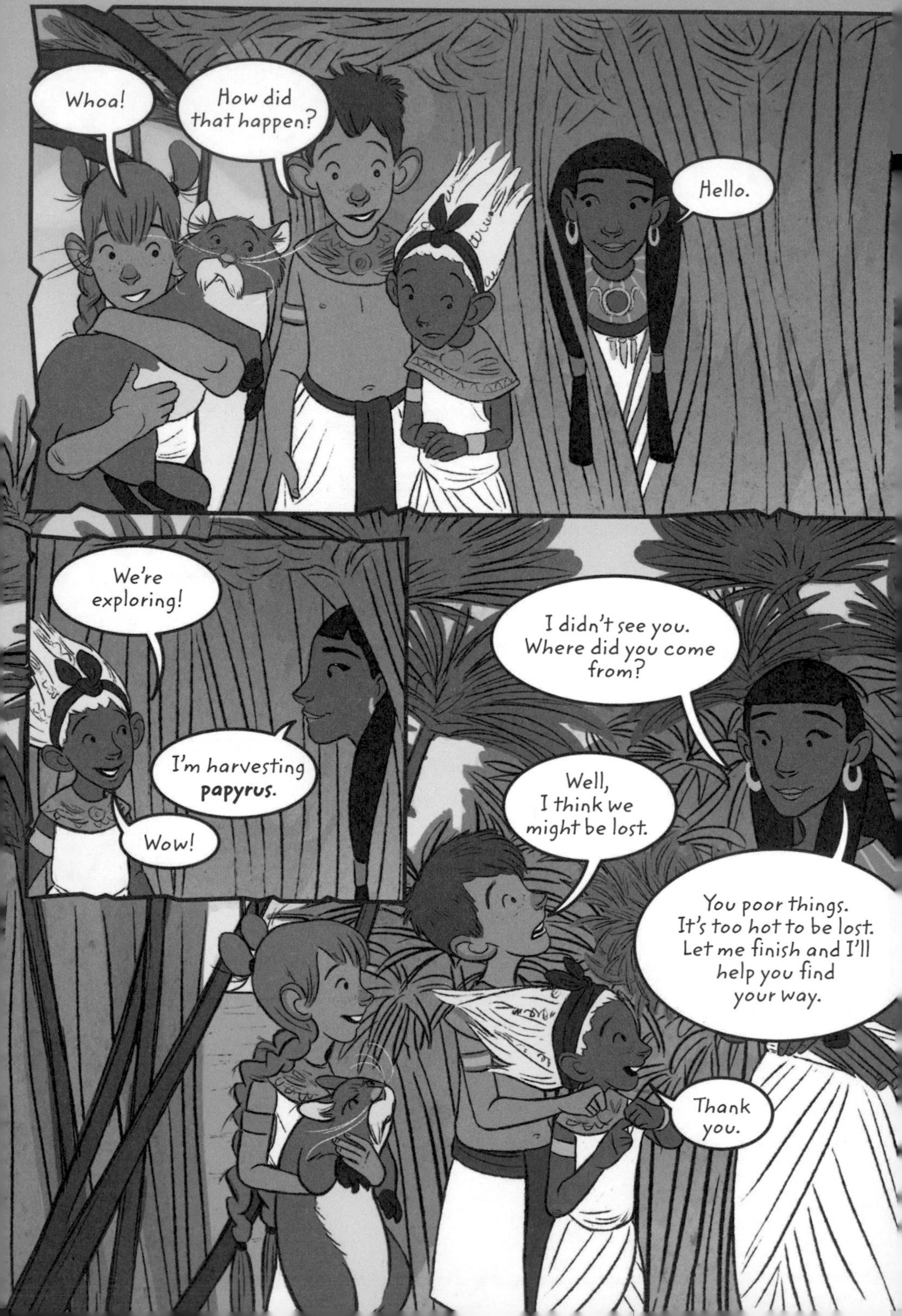
Whoa!
How did that happen?
Hello.
We're exploring!
I'm harvesting **papyrus**.
Wow!
I didn't see you. Where did you come from?
Well, I think we might be lost.
You poor things. It's too hot to be lost. Let me finish and I'll help you find your way.
Thank you.

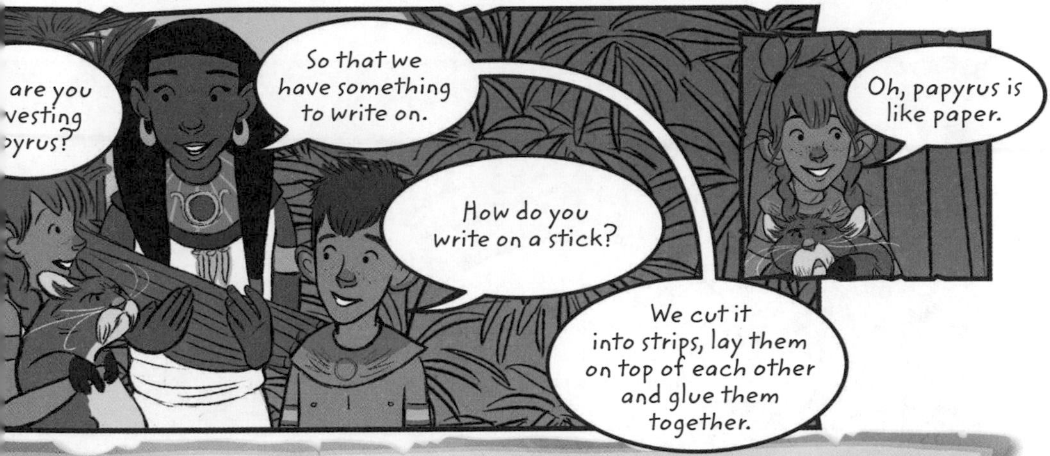
are you
vesting
yrus?
So that we have something to write on.
How do you write on a stick?
We cut it into strips, lay them on top of each other and glue them together.
Oh, papyrus is like paper.

Ancient Egyptian paper

The ancient Egyptians have made paper from papyrus since around 4000 BC.

The plant can grow up to 16 feet (4.9 m) high.

Papyrus reeds are also used to make boats, baskets, and sandals.

Even the ancient Romans used papyrus.

Parchment, made from animals' skins, eventually took the place of papyrus.

Make your own papyrus

ou will need:

- Paper
- Scissors
- Glue

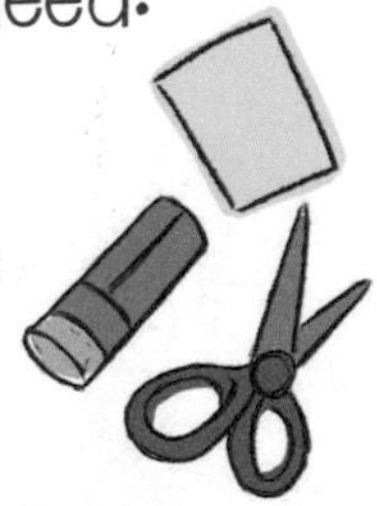

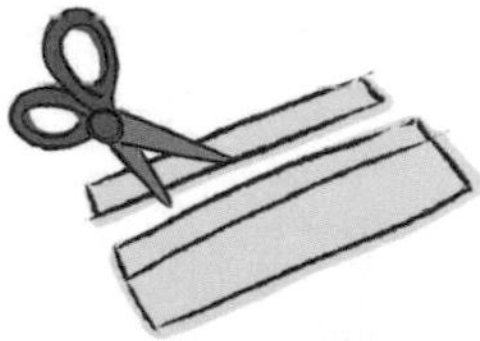

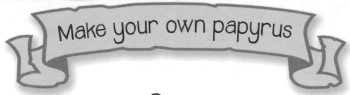

1. Imagine that the paper is a papyrus reed and cut it into strips.

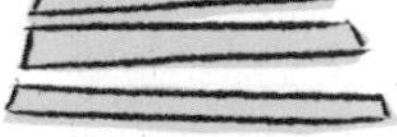

2. Lay half of the strips next to each other horizontally (side by side).

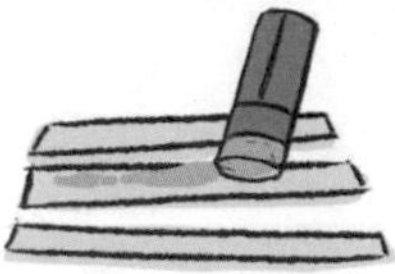

3. Cover the top side of these strips with glue.

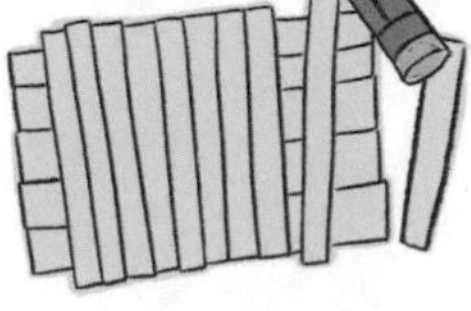

4. Take the other half of the strips and place them vertically (top to bottom) on top of the glue.

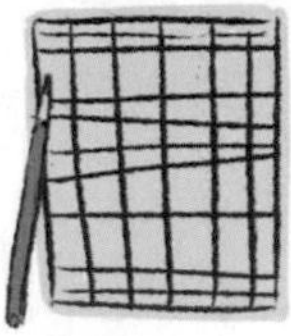

5. Wait for the glue to dry and you have your own papyrus to write on.

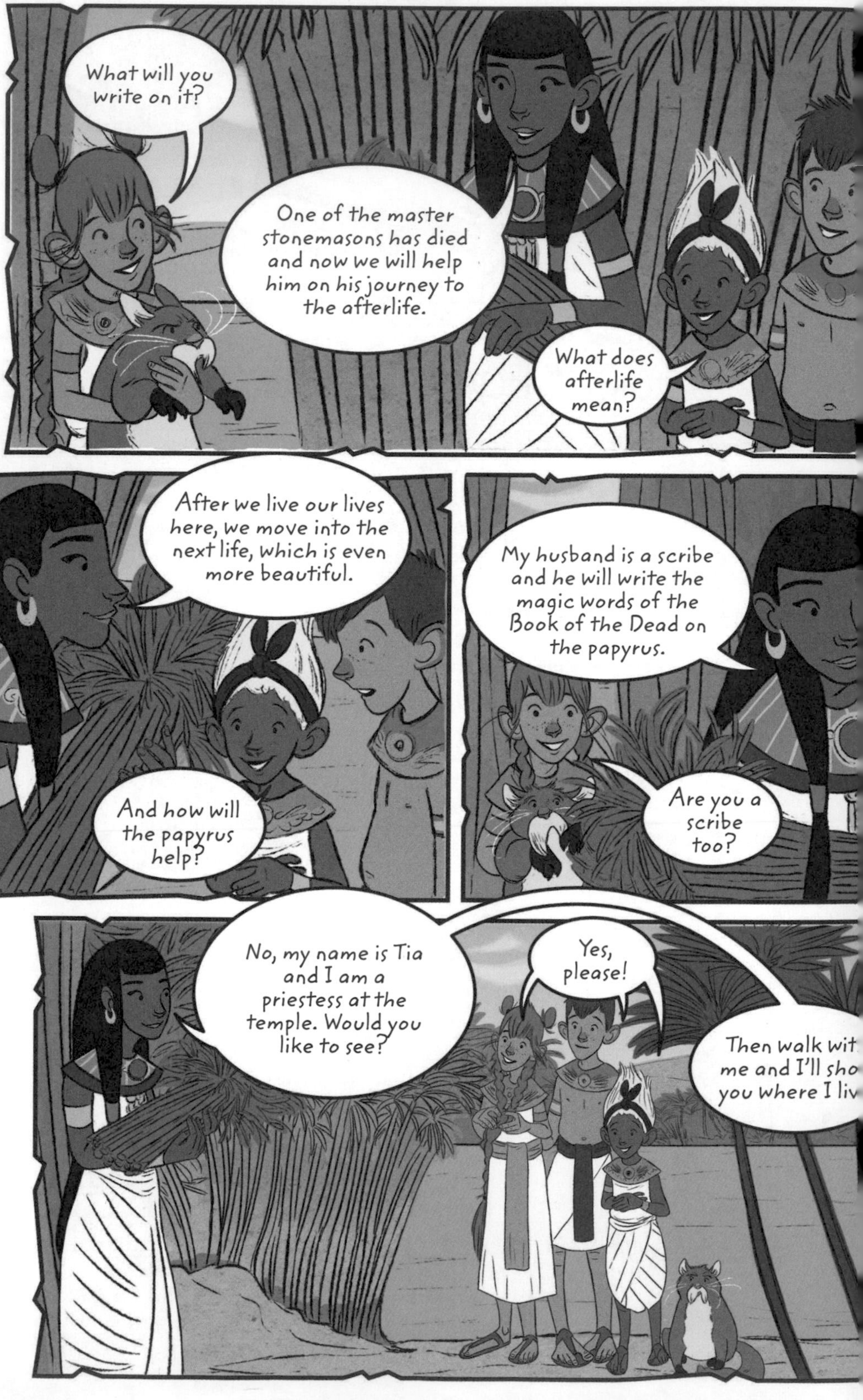
What will you write on it?
One of the master stonemasons has died and now we will help him on his journey to the afterlife.
What does afterlife mean?
After we live our lives here, we move into the next life, which is even more beautiful.
And how will the papyrus help?
My husband is a scribe and he will write the magic words of the Book of the Dead on the papyrus.
Are you a scribe too?
No, my name is Tia and I am a priestess at the temple. Would you like to see?
Yes, please!

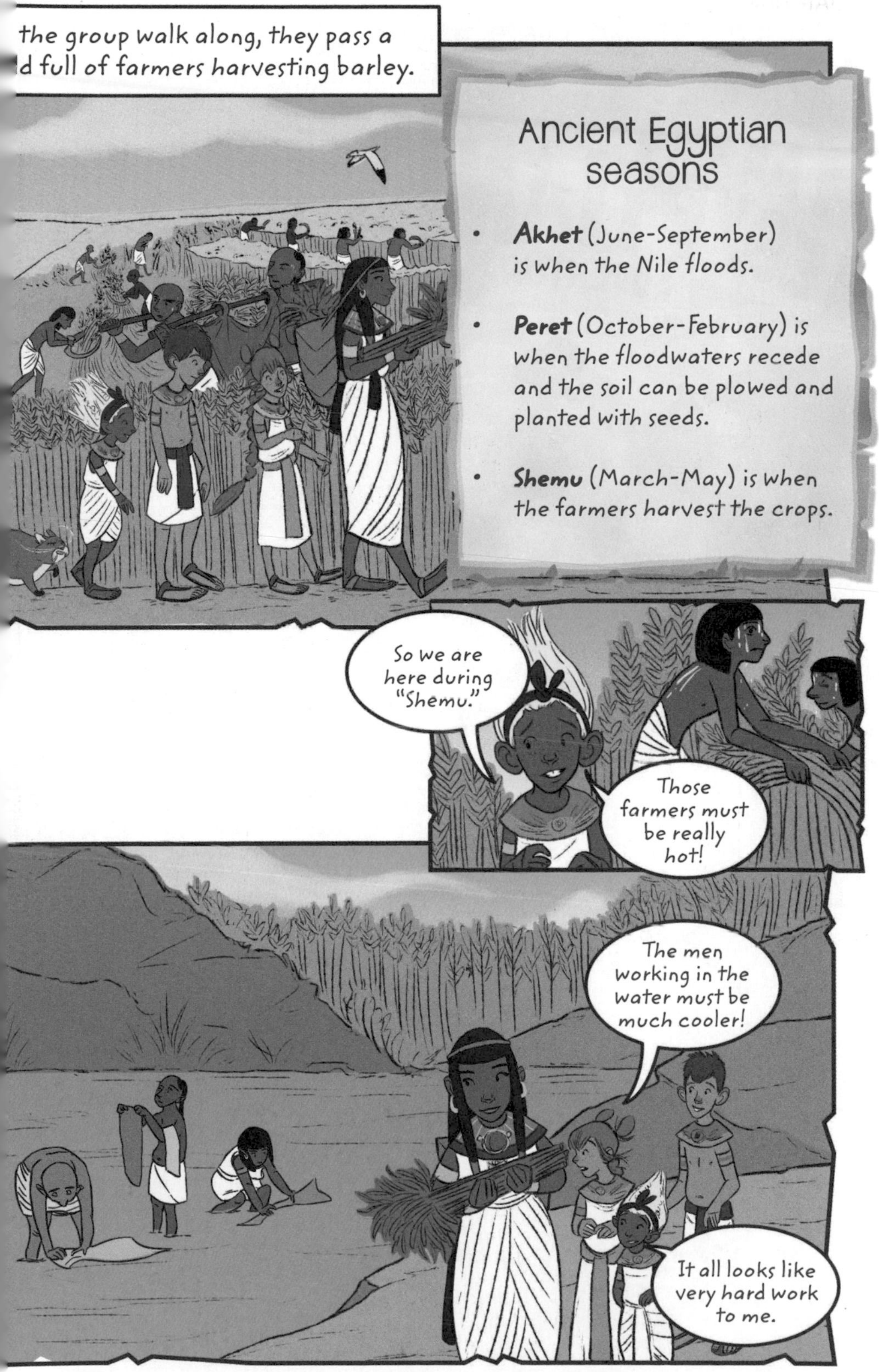
the group walk along, they pass a
d full of farmers harvesting barley.
Ancient Egyptian seasons
• **Akhet** (June-September) is when the Nile floods.
• **Peret** (October-February) is when the floodwaters recede and the soil can be plowed and planted with seeds.
• **Shemu** (March-May) is when the farmers harvest the crops.
So we are here during "Shemu."
Those farmers must be really hot!
The men working in the water must be much cooler!
It all looks like very hard work to me.